Fearless

IN
the MIX

MANDY GONZALEZ
with SUSHIL PREET K. CHEEMA

ALADDIN
New York   London   Toronto   Sydney   New Delhi

For my mom, Robin —M. G.

To my parents, for the inspiration,
and to Robert, for the encouragement —S. P. K. C.

ALADDIN | An imprint of Simon & Schuster Children's Publishing Division | 1230 Avenue of the Americas, New York, New York 10020 | First Aladdin hardcover edition April 2023 | Text copyright © 2023 by In This Together Media LLC and Mandy Gonzalez | Jacket illustration copyright © 2023 by Geraldine Rodriguez | All rights reserved, including the right of reproduction in whole or in part in any form. | ALADDIN and related logo are registered trademarks of Simon & Schuster, Inc. | For information about special discounts for bulk purchases, please contact Simon & Schuster Special Sales at 1-866-506-1949 or business@simonandschuster.com. | The Simon & Schuster Speakers Bureau can bring authors to your live event. For more information or to book an event contact the Simon & Schuster Speakers Bureau at 1-866-248-3049 or visit our website at www.simonspeakers.com. | Designed by Laura Lyn DiSiena | The text of this book was set in Bookman Old Style. | Manufactured in the United States of America 0223 FFG | 2 4 6 8 10 9 7 5 3 1 | Library of Congress Cataloging-in-Publication Data | Names: Gonzalez, Mandy, author. | Cheema, Sushil Preet K., author. Title: In the mix / by Mandy Gonzalez with Sushil Preet K. Cheema. Description: First Aladdin hardcover edition. | New York : Aladdin Books, 2023. | Series: Fearless series ; 3 | Audience: Ages 8-12. | Summary: When twelve-year-old Hudson enters a baking contest, he feels caught between his love of baking and the theater. Identifiers: LCCN 2022037021 | ISBN 9781665922012 (hardcover) | ISBN 9781665922036 (v. 3 ; ebook) Subjects: CYAC: Baking—Fiction. | Contests—Fiction. | Musicals—Fiction.\ | Theater—Fiction. | New York (N.Y.)—Fiction. Classification: LCC PZ7.1.G6523 In 2023 | DDC [Fic]—dc23 LC record available at https://lccn.loc.gov/2022037021

One

Hudson Patel blew the hair out of his eyes as he carefully removed a nearly finished Baked Alaska from the freezer. He had started his creation the previous day, when he mixed scoops of chocolate and vanilla ice cream with raspberry sorbet and then froze them before adding more ice cream and layers of pound cake to freeze overnight. This recipe wasn't necessarily the most difficult he had attempted, but it was one that required the most patience to make sure it was done just right.

Before the Baked Alaska, Hudson had already perfected other delicious treats: the Cronut (a doughnut-croissant), the famous Magnolia Bakery banana pudding, several pastries, and all kinds of cakes. But the Baked Alaska was a different level of delicious and daunting.

For the last three hours, as the meringue hardened in the freezer, Hudson had attempted to clean the kitchen. But despite his best efforts, it was still a mess, with splotches of chocolate and vanilla ice cream and raspberry sorbet stuck on every surface. The meringue he had whipped up in a mixer using egg whites and sugar was everywhere too. It was even in Hudson's hair.

Hudson started playing the FoodTube video with the recipe again. "For the last, final, most crucial step: preheat your oven to five hundred degrees so you can brown the meringue," the show's host said perkily.

"I don't have time for that!" Hudson yelled at the screen. "I've got to be at the theater soon!" Hudson had exactly an hour to get from his family's home on Manhattan's Upper West Side to the Ethel Merman Theater in Midtown, where he and his friends Monica, Relly, and April would perform in their hit Broadway show, *Our Time*. Hudson knew he couldn't afford to be late.

The FoodTube show host chimed in again, almost as if she had heard Hudson's shout of frustration. "You can also use a butane cooking torch for this last finishing touch."

Hudson's face lit up, and he rummaged through the kitchen drawer, letting the video continue playing.

"Voilà! My savior!" Hudson proclaimed as he pulled out a small butane torch specifically used for cooking. "This is what will make my viewers of *Broadway Sizzlers* really excited," he said out loud. *Broadway Sizzlers* was his own FoodTube show, which often included famous guests. Lately he had seen more and more subscribers to his channel and views on his videos, which was really exciting.

Hudson leaned closely over the Baked Alaska and lit the torch, which he had recently bought but had not yet used. He knew his parents—especially his mom—would not approve of him trying to use it without an adult present. He started carefully, turning the plate with his left hand while he used the torch with his right. Slowly, the white meringue took on a brownish tinge where the blue flame hit it.

Hudson was so engrossed in his work that he did not notice the video with the Baked Alaska recipe had ended. But what he heard next immediately caught his attention.

"Hey there, young folks and fans of FoodTube, have I got some exciting news for you!" Hudson snapped his head toward the screen at the sound of Charlie Richards's voice. Charlie was one of the most famous FoodTube stars, known for the signature cowboy hat and fringed jacket he wore. He made his name by visiting people in their home kitchens to learn about their family recipes and how to make various ethnic cuisines. "It's that time of year again—time for Bake It Till You Make It! This year, though, the competition is only open to young bakers. . . ."

Hudson was so distracted by the competition announcement that he didn't notice he had kept the torch going—he burned a hole right through the meringue and set the towel in his left hand on fire! He yelled as he felt the twinge of pain from the flames singeing his fingertips. The smoke detector went off, piercing his ears.

Hudson's mother came running from the other room, still tying a fluffy bathrobe at her waist. Her long dark hair started to fall out of the knot she had tied on top of her head (her "pineapple," as Hudson's father affectionately called it). "Hudson, what have you done this time?" she cried. The fire had interrupted her one indulgence—a late-Saturday-afternoon bath.

"Good job!" yelled his younger brother, Sudhir, who was doing his homework in the bedroom he and Hudson shared. Always focused on his science and math books, he hated to be interrupted by anything, but especially by Hudson. Hudson's baby sister, Nisha, just shy of turning one, was wailing in the next room. Fortunately, Hudson's grandmother, who had moved in with the family shortly after Hudson's grandfather died, was not at home.

Hudson's father, a quiet man who always had a twinkle

of mischief in his eyes, peered around the corner from the living room where he had been reading a novel. He laughed at the sight of his wife pouring a glass of water onto the Baked Alaska and throwing the flaming towel into the sink.

"Hudson, you should be getting ready for the theater, not setting the house on fire!" his mother scolded. Just then she spotted the butane torch and picked it up. "Where did you get this?"

"I bought it," Hudson said hesitantly, lowering his eyes to escape his mother's piercing gaze.

"You can't have something like this in the house," she said, clearly more exasperated than before. "What if your brother or sister gets ahold of it?"

"But how is it any different from the stove or the oven?" Hudson protested.

"Hudson, just go to the theater!" his mother yelled this time. "You do want a successful theater career, don't you?"

Hudson paused. His mother's words struck him in a way he had not expected. Of course he liked performing, but he really loved creating in the kitchen. The difference between this "like" and "love" was something he had been thinking about more and more lately.

"Jao, beta," Hudson's father said to Hudson quietly. "You go to the theater and have fun with your friends. I'll help your mother clean up the kitchen." He squeezed

Hudson's shoulder and ushered him toward the front door.

Hudson smiled meekly at his father and then let out a long sigh. He hated losing the Baked Alaska, but he especially hated upsetting his mom. He could still hear her muttering as he tied his shoes: "We're having a big feast soon for Diwali. He can't make any more messes in here."

Hudson realized that, in all the chaos, he had missed most of Charlie Richards's announcement on FoodTube. He made a mental note to find it later. He put on his blue windbreaker and grabbed his backpack as his father clicked the kitchen TV to the local news.

As the door to the house closed behind him, Hudson heard another announcement: "There's a new Broadway show opening soon, just down the street from the super-hit musical *Our Time*. . . ."

"What?" Hudson said aloud in the hallway to no one. He wanted to run back inside to hear the rest of the segment, but after glancing at his phone, he saw that he really had to hustle. "I need to get to the theater!"

He punched at the button on the elevator repeatedly, but it was as slow as ever. Instead, he ran down the ornate hallway, lined with fine antiques and burgundy carpet, to the stairs. He made it down four flights as quickly as he could.

Hudson burst onto the sidewalk but stopped short at the sight before him. The sun was setting, and the sky above Riverside Park was glowing strawberry red and eggplant purple. Many leaves on the trees were pumpkin orange and squash yellow, just in time for fall.

Hudson took a moment to admire the different hues. Then he ran as fast as he could toward the subway station on West Eighty-Sixth Street—to another Saturday night on Broadway.

Two

The subway ride on the 1 train was not long, but it was busy and crowded. At Seventy-Second Street, Hudson had jumped off and rushed across the platform in hopes that one of the express trains would get him to Midtown faster. But when he peered down the subway tracks, he did not see the light of an incoming train. He barely made it back onto the local before the doors closed; in the process, he jostled a middle-aged woman dressed finely in an olive-green gown, one fine enough for a night at the opera in Lincoln Center. She huffed at Hudson when she dropped her beaded clutch on the subway floor.

"So sorry, ma'am!" Hudson said. It seemed that his

body was becoming more and more unwieldy these days, par for the course for a thirteen-year-old boy who was growing quickly.

The woman shot Hudson another angry look as she exited the subway car at her stop—Sixty-Sixth Street.

Why is she even on the train if she's so fancy? Hudson thought. But he knew why—it was one of the reasons he loved the city so much. Anyone and everyone mixed together in the various neighborhoods and on the train, which ran all night. It was true that the city never slept.

At Fifty-Ninth Street, Columbus Circle, a family of four got on the train. One of the kids, a young girl, kept looking in Hudson's direction until he smiled at her and waved. She giggled and hid her face behind her hands, then tugged at her father's jacket until he leaned down to hear what she had to say. She whispered in his ear and then pointed in Hudson's direction.

The father looked over at Hudson too and then walked over. "Excuse me," he said quietly, "but are you Hudson Patel of *Broadway Sizzlers*?"

Hudson nodded and flashed a smile. He was getting recognized more and more often for his FoodTube show rather than his role in *Our Time.*

"My daughter is a huge fan," the man continued. "Could she have your autograph and a picture?"

"Of course," Hudson said. He posed with the shy girl and signed his name on a small notebook her mother found in her handbag.

"Thanks for watching *Broadway Sizzlers*," Hudson said. "And if you haven't already, check out my Broadway show, *Our Time*, at the Ethel Merman Theater. I play Crash!" He waved at the family as they settled into seats that opened up as the train made its way to the next stop.

Finally, the train arrived in Times Square, Forty-Second Street, the center of the world, particularly to Hudson, the Squad, and other Broadway stars. Millions of tourists flocked to this very spot in the Big Apple every year to see the magnificent city and experience its magic. It was practically a requirement to see at least one Broadway show as a visitor, and, as much as he despised the crowds when he was in a rush (like right now), Hudson appreciated that the people were there to support the arts and shows like his.

Hudson raced under the bright neon lights shining from the marquees (like *Wicked*, one of his all-time favorites) and dodged crowds as best he could to get to the Ethel Merman Theater.

"Good to see you," said Jimmy Onions, the theater's beloved stage-door doorman, tipping his hat as Hudson caught his breath.

"I made it!" Hudson was relieved.

"You've got time to spare," said Jimmy, who had worked at the theater for nearly forty-five years. He used his security camera to keep track of the comings and goings around the theater, but he knew its rhythms so well that he could recite the call times and show times by heart.

"But you know I've been having trouble with my costume. I don't want my pants to split again like they did on opening night." Hudson cringed at the memory while he quickly signed the call-board.

Jimmy laughed and bit into a shiny green apple. "Have a good show!" He watched as Hudson nearly tripped on his way to the dressing rooms.

Just inside the door, Hudson ran into Monica Garcia and April DaSilva, his castmates. April was untangling hair from Monica's wig from the buttons on the back of her dress. The two girls were singing scales to warm up their voices.

"You're off-key," Hudson joked as he rushed past his friends and disappeared into the dressing room he shared with Relly Morton.

"Are we?" Monica wondered aloud.

"No, silly," said April. "He's just messing with us. As usual."

The four friends made up the Squad, which was the name the show's director, Artie Hoffman, had given them. In addition to performing together, they sometimes found themselves on adventures. Monica, the only one in the group from outside the tristate area, had relocated to Brooklyn from California with her abuelita to follow her Broadway dreams. Nearly a year earlier, she had led the Squad in saving the Ethel Merman from a decades-long curse. It had nearly derailed the show, but now *Our Time* had become one of the biggest hits Broadway had ever seen.

More recently, the four friends had traveled back in time and discovered why Relly's grandfather was hesitant to let Relly become a full-time performer and dancer. With a lot of determination and a little magic, they helped Grandpa Slyde improve his own life *and* convinced him to fully support Relly's dreams. They also got to know Harlem's rich history in the arts and even Ethel Merman's story—really well, in fact.

Through it all, April—and increasingly, the rest of the Squad—documented everything for social media, complete with hashtags and behind-the-scenes videos, which her growing group of followers loved.

But right now—this moment—was no time for adventure. It was nearing the start of the show. Hudson only had a few minutes to change.

"What's all this white stuff?" Relly asked as Hudson pulled on his costume. He reached over to pick white chunks out of the hair that was again falling into Hudson's eyes. "Eww, it's sticky!"

Hudson took a close look in the mirror. "Must be the meringue."

"The what?"

"Meringue. It's a mix of egg whites, cream of tartar, and sugar that was the final layer of the Baked Alaska."

"The what?" Relly said again. Relly loved Hudson's desserts, but he often had no idea what they were now that Hudson was experimenting more and more with advanced recipes. It wasn't all just cookies anymore.

"It's a dessert with different types of ice cream . . . ," Hudson began as he tried to get the bits of meringue out of his hair. But Relly wasn't listening.

"What kind of cookies did you bring us today?" he asked, a huge grin on his face as he rubbed his hands together excitedly. He did a twirl and tapped his feet. The talented dancer could never sit still. He paused and leaned in closer to Hudson. "And why do your fingertips look burned?"

"Just a little accident in the kitchen. And, shoot, I forgot the treats!" Hudson groaned. "They were good ones, too—strawberry macarons. I think I finally figured out how to make them without breaking the delicate shells."

"Ah, you forgot the treats!" Relly exclaimed, feigning anguish as he threw his head back and clutched at his stomach. "I have no idea what a macaron is, but you know strawberry is my favorite!"

Three loud knocks interrupted the boys. "Are you ready? It's almost time to go on!" It was the stage manager, Claudia Middleton, who had impeccable timing and made sure that everything at the Ethel Merman, including the cast, ran like clockwork.

Relly flung the door open and stepped out. "Hi, Claudia," he said.

"Hudson, what have you done to your hair?" Claudia said, stepping toward him and reaching out her hands. "It's sticking out in every direction at the front!"

"It's the meringue," Relly said from the doorway as April and Monica peeked their heads in to see what the fuss was all about. Sure enough, pieces of Hudson's hair were sticking straight out, just like the spikes on the Statue of Liberty's crown.

"I don't know what you're talking about," Claudia said. She ushered the kids into the hallway. Hudson ran to the wig room, where Chris was waiting with Hudson's wig cap in hand. He tried to smooth down Hudson's hair.

"I'm not sure it will stay on," Chris said to no one in particular. He fitted the curly wig on top of the cap. "We'll just have to hope it doesn't fall off. I don't have time to do anything more." He glanced at Claudia, but she had already lost interest in Hudson's hair. She checked her watch and motioned for Hudson to join the rest of the Squad.

"You've all warmed up, I hope?" Claudia asked.

"Yes," said April and Monica. Relly nodded.

"Hudson?" Claudia said. "Are you paying attention?"

"I'm ready," Hudson said.

"But not warmed up." It was a statement, not a question.

Hudson simply looked at his shoes.

But the show had to go on, as always.

"Hudson, what kind of cookies did you make for us today?" one of the stagehands asked as the Squad made its way toward the stage.

"Macarons," Relly said in his best imitation of a French accent. "Strawberry macarons. But he forgot to bring them."

The stagehand was upset. So was April.

"What will we snack on at intermission?" she asked desperately, snapping one last selfie before showtime. "Hashtag No Cookies," she said as she uploaded the photo to Instagram. She added a "scream" emoji before Claudia snatched the phone away.

"My phone!" April exclaimed.

"You can have it back after the show," Claudia said.

Moments later, the kids were onstage, under the bright lights. Hudson was clearly distracted. Going on cold was never a good idea. He tripped over his feet more than once and was slightly off-key in one group song. His wig started to slide just before intermission, but Chris was able to secure it before the second act.

Fortunately, the audience members didn't notice any near mishaps. They were just happy to have the chance to see the hottest show in town.

At curtain call, the cast came out to bow and bask in the roaring applause. This was usually one of the Squad's favorite parts of the show, but tonight Monica, Relly, and April could tell that Hudson was ready to be finished for the night.

"Hey, Hudson, what was that all about?" Relly said as they cleared the stage. The hum of the excited audience followed them to the back of the theater.

Hudson shook his head. "I don't know. I just made a few mistakes," he muttered. He knew he was not the show's strongest dancer (that honor went to Relly), its strongest singer (that was Monica), or even its strongest actor (that was April). But he had charisma and charm that the audience loved. Lately, though, performing was more challenging than usual.

But baking didn't let him down. Even when things got messy like they had earlier, he was usually able to pull off a perfect ending. And if he did mess up, he could always start over. His FoodTube fans even loved seeing his mishaps—they made the experience more real. On top of having a steady stream of new followers and views, Hudson was increasingly getting emails and messages about other sponsorships that had nothing to do with *Our Time*—they were about *Broadway Sizzlers*.

That was why he needed to know more about Bake It Till You Make It.

Finally, the Squad made it back to the dressing rooms on the second floor of the theater. Hudson rummaged through his navy backpack until he found his phone.

He tried typing "Bake It Till You Make It competition" into the search engine. But April, still bitter about Claudia taking her phone away before the show, snatched it from him. "Hudson, what's going on with you?"

"Tell us what's up," said Monica, ever calm and patient. She walked to the wall and straightened a framed cover of *People* magazine that featured the Squad. UNDERDOGS OF BROADWAY, the headline read. That article, published a few months earlier, had boosted the Squad's popularity. Now all four friends were quickly getting used to the fame and attention.

Hudson let out a big sigh. "I was making a Baked Alaska at home—" he began, but Relly cut him off.

"I still don't know what that is, or what that stuff is in your hair," Relly said.

"That's beside the point," Monica said, hushing him.

"The last step involves browning the meringue," Hudson continued. "I didn't have time to do it in the oven, so I used a butane torch—"

"A butane torch!" Relly interrupted again. He jumped to his feet and perfectly executed the slide his grandpa Gregory had taught him. "I didn't know you got to use a torch in cooking! Maybe I should learn."

"Relly, focus!" April scolded her friend.

Hudson continued. "I set off the fire alarm, waking my baby sister and interrupting my mom's bath. She was really upset." He paused. He hated upsetting his mom, especially knowing how much she enjoyed a good bath.

"You could buy her some bath bombs to make up for it," April suggested. "Or you could give her bath salts."

But Hudson wasn't listening. He was staring at his shoes, clearly thinking about something else.

"There's more, isn't there?" Monica said. She stepped closer to her friend. "What's going on?"

But before Hudson could tell his friends about Charlie Richards and the Bake It Till You Make It announcement, Jimmy appeared.

"It's time to meet your fans!" he shouted cheerily.

The Squad eagerly followed him to the stage door.

"Ready?" Jimmy was grinning.

The four friends instinctively reached for each other's hands and smiled, ready for one of their other favorite parts of the show: meeting their fans.

"Ready!"

Jimmy flung the door open, revealing a large crowd held back by metal barricades. Flashes from smartphone cameras blinded them.

"Hey, Hudson, did you hear the news about the Bake It Till You Make It competition?" Jimmy shouted over the roar of the crowd. "And did all of you hear about the new show down the street?"

Monica, Relly, April, and Hudson all turned to ask what he was talking about, but Jimmy was suddenly preoccupied with an overzealous fan who was trying to climb over a barricade.

Soon enough, the kids were absorbed by their work with the crowd too.

Three

The Squad spent a full thirty minutes signing autographs and posing for selfies. They got so caught up in the task at hand and in the excitement of the crowd that they nearly forgot what Jimmy Onions had said—all but Hudson, that is. Hudson was eager as ever to find out the details of the competition he had heard about on FoodTube. And he wanted to know if Jimmy was talking about that new show he had heard about on the news as he rushed out of his home and to the theater.

He tried to get closer to Jimmy to talk, but the crowd was particularly boisterous this evening; Jimmy was having a tough time keeping it under control. It was easy for

Hudson to step away from the crowd: many fans were dressed up as Pax, Tony, and Froggie—Relly's, Monica's, and April's characters—but fewer were dressed as Crash. So Hudson found a spot as far away from the crowd as possible and began searching his pockets.

"Shoot, April still has my phone!" he muttered to himself. He glanced in April's direction and spotted the blue case sticking out of a pocket on her denim jacket. He quietly made his way over to her and gently slid the phone out of her pocket as she took a picture with yet another fan.

"Come here, Hudson. Join the picture!" April said, drawing him in close, oblivious to his surreptitious act.

Hudson flashed his biggest smile and signed a few more autographs before putting his pen away. The crowd was thinning. Jimmy and the stagehands were dispersing the remaining fans.

"These kids have to get home, you know," one of the stagehands said. "If they kept signing and taking pictures, they'd be here all night."

The last of the fans were hardly gone when Hudson whipped out his phone and again typed in, "Bake It Till You Make It competition." Finally, he found the information he wanted.

At the top of the page was a banner featuring Charlie, again in his usual brown cowboy hat, fringed leather jacket, and coordinating cowboy boots.

"Oh my gosh!" Hudson exclaimed. "I can enter!"

"What's up?" Monica asked, peering over Hudson's shoulder at the glowing screen. "Enter what?"

"The Bake It Till You Make It competition! It's open to kids only this year, and you have to be younger than fifteen to participate."

"Wait. Tell me more," April said as she hit record on her phone, sensing that something important was about to happen. "Ready, action!"

"Charlie Richards, who's a huge star on FoodTube, is hosting the competition this year. It's open to kids under the age of fifteen only. And we have to make"—Hudson paused as he kept scrolling down the page—"cupcakes?"

"Oh wow, Hudson, that's so exciting!" Monica said. "You have to enter!"

"Yes, you do," echoed Relly. "But only if I get to try everything you make—as usual."

Hudson didn't respond immediately. He was still reading the details of the competition on his phone. Then his eyes fell to the ground again.

"What's wrong now?" April asked, frustrated. "You can't look so sad in a video on social media, you know, Hudson."

"I don't know if my parents are going to like this," Hudson said.

"Like what?" Relly asked.

"Me entering the competition. Not after what happened today. Setting off the fire alarm while baking and then asking if I can enter the biggest baking competition ever is probably not going to go over well."

"But what does the winner get?" April wanted to know.

Hudson looked at the screen again. "Nothing my parents are going to want me to have, not with all the other stuff that keeps me so busy."

"What is it, though?" Monica asked gently.

Hudson sighed for the third time that night. "A kiosk in the center of Times Square, where I can sell the cupcake next summer."

"What!" Monica, Relly, and April roared at the same time. They were so loud that they startled several passersby on the street.

"Hudson, you have to at least submit an application," Monica said. "See what happens. You're such a talented baker. It would be terrible to see you let such a great opportunity slip by!"

His friends' encouragement gave Hudson confidence; his posture straightened out under the weight of his backpack.

"Okay, you got me," Hudson said. "But I'm hungry. Where shall we go to eat tonight?"

"Well, I know what I want," Relly said. "Dessert for

dinner. All this talk about cupcakes and baking has got my sweet tooth acting up, and I bet your little brother is eating the strawberry macarons that were meant for us."

The Squad started walking away from the Ethel Merman.

"Just to be clear, where are we going?" Monica asked. "I should text my abuelita so she knows where we'll be."

"We're going to Serendipity 3, of course!" Hudson said.

"Ooh, I want a Frrrozen Hot Chocolate," said April, already plotting hashtags for her *#DessertforDinner* pictures and videos.

"'It does all sorts of things to your mouth!'" the Squad said in unison, quoting a waiter they had met at the famed eatery shortly after the *People* article was published.

April, Hudson, and Relly were chatting away excitedly when they noticed that Monica had fallen behind. She had stopped on the sidewalk and was squinting at a poster under an unlit awning. It was the Broadhurst Theatre, which had been closed for a long time. The Squad regularly walked by it and hadn't paid it any attention at all.

"What is it, Monica?" Relly asked as he, April, and Hudson walked back toward her.

Monica took a sharp breath. "What was it Jimmy said about a new show opening?"

"I heard about it on the news," Hudson said, "but I didn't get the full scoop."

Now all four friends were looking closely at the poster.

Sure enough, the poster, freshly printed and not yet worn, was an announcement for an upcoming show.

"It's a musical called *Move It!*, directed by world-renowned puppeteer Alexa Lopez!" April shouted. "I bet it's going to be fabulous!" She stepped closer for a better look but then leapt back quickly. "Wait! 'It stars a group of kids dressed as animals and features that will delight the entire audience,'" she read aloud from the poster. Her mood abruptly changed. "How is this possible?"

"I bet my brother would love that," Monica said. She and her younger brother, Freddy, who lived in California with their parents, were very close.

"He can't love this show!" April snapped. "What about *our* show? Remember—we're the cute kids on Broadway. This is *our time*. Literally!" She was so upset that her friends took a step back.

They all stood silently for a few moments.

"Do you all still want to go to Serendipity 3?" Hudson finally asked his friends. Dessert always made things better. Right?

Before they knew it, April had hailed a cab to save them from a long walk.

"Move over, Hudson! I'm crushed against the window," Relly complained from the back seat.

"I can't move any more," Hudson shouted back, over April and Monica, who sat between them.

"One of you has to sit in the front," April said. "Monica and I are squished."

"I'll go up front," Hudson said. "I'm the oldest."

"You're also the biggest," said Relly. Hudson had always been big-boned, but Relly had noticed his friend's recent growth spurt.

Once everyone was settled into the cab, the driver took off, oblivious to the amount of Broadway fame in his car. The radio played reggaeton music, and a Jamaican flag hung from the rearview mirror.

"Wait!" April, now seated by the window, shouted to no one in particular.

The driver slammed on the brakes. "What's wrong, miss?" he said, turning around with concern to look at her.

But April just pointed at the radio. She was speechless. A news segment was playing.

"Can you please turn up the volume?" Monica asked the driver.

He nodded and turned the dial before he started driving again. Everyone in the taxi was quiet as they listened to the radio.

"The new show is called *Move It!* and will star young Tabitha Fox, who was originally cast for the role of Tony in

Our Time, but she left that production to star in the huge television hit *The Adventure Begins*. She's broken out as one of the biggest new faces in show business."

Relly, Hudson, and April turned toward Monica, who closed her eyes as she listened to the rest of the segment. Finally, the reggaeton music started up again.

"Tabitha's got nothing on us—any of us," Relly said. "She may have been the original pick for your role in *Our Time*, Monica, but she ran out on the cast. *Twice*."

Monica was quiet. Her eyes were still closed

"Relly's right, Monica," Hudson said. "You proved yourself. You even saved the Ethel Merman. And now we're the biggest show on Broadway!"

"For now." April sighed. Hudson and Relly both threw her an annoyed look.

Soon the taxi rolled up to Serendipity 3, famous for decadent desserts the size of your head. Hudson figured a trip here would cheer them all up. Reservations were difficult to come by, but the famous Squad had never had a problem getting in, especially since they'd been featured in *People* magazine.

As usual, a crowd was at the door. Nevertheless, the Squad nudged its way to the front of the line to talk to the host, a young man who knew them well.

"There's currently a ninety-minute wait for a table of

any size," the host said, not bothering to look up from the paper in front of him.

"But it's us, the Squad from *Our Time*. Maybe you can get us in sooner?" Relly said.

The host glanced up for a moment. "Sorry, kids," he said, more kindly. "The place is jam-packed tonight. Tabitha Fox and a few other members of the new Broadway show *Move It!* are here, and everyone is trying to get a piece of them before it even starts previews." The host looked at his watch. "But they've been here a while and may be leaving soon. Let me check." He disappeared into the restaurant, which was decorated with colorful, whimsical chandeliers.

"Tabitha Fox is here?" Relly cringed.

"It's so something she would do," April said, rolling her eyes. "She loves to steal the spotlight—and the show is hardly in rehearsals!"

"And it's so busy that they can't find us a table?" Hudson wondered.

Monica, who had been very quiet since they heard the news segment in the taxi, spoke up softly. "She has been on that TV show for a while now. And she's really good. Having a TV fan base will make her Broadway show more popular, won't it?"

"But we're already the biggest show in town," Relly reminded his friends.

A familiar voice broke into the Squad's conversation. "Well, if it isn't the kids from the cursed Ethel Merman's *Our Time!*" It was Tabitha Fox. She flipped her long auburn hair away and walked directly up to Monica. The two girls, both tall for their age, stood eye-to-eye. April pulled at Monica's hand as she started to twirl her hair, a nervous habit she had nearly broken once she saved the Ethel Merman Theater and became a Broadway star.

"The Ethel Merman is not cursed," Monica said firmly.

"In case you haven't heard, *Our Time* is doing really well," Relly said, sliding up beside Monica. Not yet thirteen, he was slightly smaller than Tabitha, but his ferocity made up for anything he lacked in size. "And we're doing well— *without you.*"

Tabitha ignored him. She turned to Hudson. "What was it that *People* reporter wrote? 'Relly Morton's dancing is impeccable, April DaSilva's acting skills are ambitious, Monica Garcia's singing voice is angelic, and Hudson Patel provides the . . . *comic relief.*'" She laughed. "It sounded like they were struggling to understand why you're in that show—or on Broadway at all."

"Hudson's talented!" April nearly shouted. "His acting is great. And he's enthusiastic!"

But Tabitha, trailed by her castmates, was already on her way out of the restaurant.

April looked defeated. Relly was clenching his fists. Monica had turned bright red. But Hudson wasn't even listening; instead, he was carefully reviewing a copy of the menu.

The host had returned, ready to seat the Squad. "Kids, I have a table open!"

"No, thank you," Monica answered before leading her friends to the door. She had to pull the menu out of Hudson's hands.

Outside, April broke down.

"It's a new Squad!" April burst out, nearly in tears. "And they're led by Tabitha Fox! What are we going to do? We have . . . *competition!* They're going to be dressed as animals! We might not be the best, most fun, most lovable group of kids on Broadway anymore!"

Relly and Monica fell silent. Monica put her arm around April, who was now openly sobbing, and Relly put his hand on April's shoulder.

Suddenly, they all turned to Hudson, who was standing away from the group. The screen of his phone was lighting up his face again.

"What did you find out?" April said, trying to look at Hudson's phone. "Who are they? Who are the newbies in the cast?"

But Hudson wasn't looking up information on the *Move*

It! cast—he was looking up the recipe for a banana and lime soufflé. Soufflés were tricky—it was easy to make a huge mess (something like the disaster with the Baked Alaska earlier in the day), but if done right, they were impressive. And the banana and lime flavors would surprise anyone. . . .

"You're looking at SOUFFLÉS?" April gasped, nearly pushing Hudson away. "Aren't you concerned, Hudson? Our days as the biggest stars on Broadway could be numbered!"

She glared at Hudson. When she didn't get a response, she whipped out her own phone to look up the new show on *all* the social media platforms.

"You know, it's getting late," Hudson said awkwardly. "I'm going home. I'll see you all later."

He quickly turned away, leaving his friends speechless.

Four

Hudson took his time walking several blocks north before deciding to hop on the Seventy-Second Street bus, which would take him home to the Upper West Side. When it arrived, the advertisement plastered on its side caught his eye: it was an advertisement for *Move It!*, complete with a giant picture of Tabitha and the other kids in the cast. Stung by Tabitha's comment about his purpose in the show, he shook his head and climbed aboard. He grabbed a seat and popped in his earbuds, eager to watch the FoodTube ad for the cupcake competition in full. He pulled up the video. Once again, Charlie Richards appeared on-screen.

"Hey there, young folks and fans of FoodTube, have I

got some exciting news for you!" Charlie began again in his relaxed, casual tone. "It's that time of year again—time for Bake It Till You Make It. This year, though, the competition is only open to young bakers under the age of fifteen. To enter, you simply have to submit a short video of yourself making one of your favorite desserts. It can be anything you choose. Simple is fine, so long as you show skill and effort. But the selected finalists will be tasked with making something very specific: cupcakes.

"I'll be your host—and your judge. But this is not your typical baking competition: The finalists will be asked to put a twist on taste, create their own signature, but with one very specific guideline that I'll reveal later. Till next time."

Charlie tipped his hat at the camera in typical cowboy fashion. Then the screen went blank.

Hudson leaned back in the blue plastic seat and slumped against the bus window. He closed his eyes in defeat, shutting out Central Park passing by outside.

Well, there goes that, he thought. *I only know how to make other people's recipes.*

Soon enough, Hudson was back on the Upper West Side. He got off at Broadway and Seventy-Second Street and started walking north, happy to be in his neighborhood. He walked just a couple of blocks before finding himself at Fairway Market, a grocery store that was open late. His stomach suddenly rumbled; he realized he hadn't eaten anything since the morning.

Hudson went inside the store and wandered the aisles, looking for something that seemed appetizing. After hearing the rules for the Bake It Till You Make It competition, he'd lost his appetite for dessert for dinner. Finally, he settled on a premade sandwich. He found one of his favorites: smoked salmon.

"The perfect comfort food," Hudson said.

On his way to the register, a box piled high with fruit caught his eye.

"Mangoes!" he exclaimed. "Mom's favorite." He started squeezing the fruits with his free hand to find ones that were not too ripe and not yet past their prime. He ultimately found three that were just right. *I'll surprise her at breakfast tomorrow*, he thought. *I just hope she's not still upset about the Baked Alaska.*

Not wanting to disturb his family, Hudson sat on the steps of the building his family lived in and quickly devoured his smoked salmon sandwich. After tossing the wrapper in a nearby trash can, he slumped up the four flights of stairs, each step heavier than the next.

Once he reached the landing, he took a deep breath

before before entering his family home. He braced himself for the inevitable squeak the heavy red door would make. He was amazed when it didn't make a sound. He was even more startled to find his mother sitting at the counter in the kitchen. Her fluffy robe was tied tightly over her mint-green pajamas, and a newspaper was open in front of her. She was digging into a bowl of ice cream. She seemed just as surprised to see Hudson as he was to see her.

"The door," Hudson said. "What's wrong with it?" The door had squeaked for as long as he could remember.

Hudson's mother laughed. "Well, nothing anymore. Your father finally fixed it. He always gets around to fixing something when he knows I'm upset," she said, tilting her head toward her son.

Hudson cringed, afraid of the lecture that was coming.

But there was no lecture. His mother simply winked at him and then grinned, the spoon facedown over her tongue.

Hudson couldn't help but sigh with relief. He set the bag of mangoes on the counter and untied his shoes. He hung his backpack and his jacket on a hook by the door. He watched as his mother undid her ponytail, flipped her head over, and then tied another "pineapple"—a messy knot on the top of her head. A.R. Rahman's biggest hits played in the background.

"You're up late," Hudson said. His mother usually went

to bed by nine p.m., even on a Saturday night, unless there was a special occasion.

"I couldn't sleep," she said. "The lingering smell of burnt towel made me crave ice cream, sorbet, and cake." She tilted her bowl toward Hudson so he could get a better look at what she was eating.

"Is that the Baked Alaska?" he asked, surprised and excited all at once.

"It's *remnants* of the Baked Alaska. I had to scrape off the burnt meringue. But you did a good job. I'm always impressed by your baking skills."

Hudson beamed with pride and ran his fingers through his still sticky hair.

"How was the show tonight?" his mother asked, taking a bite of raspberry sorbet with a piece of pound cake. Now Hudson frowned.

"What happened?" his mother asked, concerned. "Is everyone okay?"

"Everyone's fine," Hudson began. "Well, sort of. It was a very . . . eventful night."

"'Eventful.'" Hudson's mother raised an eyebrow at him, eyeing her son curiously. "What happened that made it 'eventful'?"

Hudson wasn't sure where to start. Should he tell his mother about the cupcake competition, or should he start with the news about the new production of *Move It!*? Since he had already decided not to enter the competition, he told her about the new production instead.

"Oh, *Move It!*" his mother interjected. "Your father and I saw that on the news. It looks like it will be a great show. The cast is young and seems talented. It should be very cute."

"That's the problem," Hudson interrupted. "The cast is young and talented—they could be the next big thing on Broadway and take over our spotlight. We went to Serendipity 3 after the show and couldn't get a table because Tabitha Fox and some other cast members were there. They usually let us right in, but tonight we had to wait."

"Tabitha Fox is pretty famous with kids your age, right? That's what Sudhir said."

Hudson rolled his eyes. Of course his little brother would bring that up. "Yeah, she's the one who was supposed to play Tony in *Our Time* at first."

"But then she claimed the theater was dangerous and even haunted, right?" Hudson's mother shook her head and took another bite of ice cream.

"Yeah, that was her. After we saw Tabitha, Monica, Relly, and April were really upset—especially April—but I was really hungry. I guess I didn't see it as that big a deal at the time," Hudson continued.

Hudson's mother eyed him carefully from beneath her pineapple bun, which was starting to fall over a bit.

"So, food is more concerning to you than a new show that could upend your theater career," she said, punctuating every other word with a tap of her spoon on the side of the ice cream bowl. It was a statement, not a question.

Hudson was silent. He wasn't sure what to say. He suddenly felt vulnerable. If he didn't move, he thought for a moment, maybe he wouldn't have to answer.

"Hudson," his mother said gently after a long pause, "you should enter that baking competition."

"I can't," Hudson burst out. "I don't know what I'll make." He paused, looking at his mother suspiciously. "Wait, how did you know about the competition?"

His mother smiled sneakily back at him. "You're not the only one who likes to watch FoodTube, beta," she said. "And what do you mean you can't enter? You can make anything. Even this Baked Alaska would have been pretty perfect if you hadn't been distracted."

Hudson wanted to explain to his mother the rules of the competition—that there would be a surprise twist for the final competition, yet to be revealed. And that he'd have to make an original recipe. But he didn't know how to explain his frustration, particularly to his mom. Instead, he was silent, staring at the floor.

"Get some rest, Hudson," his mother said, putting her hand on his shoulder. "You've had a very busy day. And tomorrow you should make some special cookies for your friends. Your father and brother ate all those strawberry macarons you forgot today."

"I hope they liked them," Hudson said. "Did you like them?"

"I didn't get to eat any; that's why I've got the remnants of the Baked Alaska," she said.

"Well, these are for you too—a special treat. I was going to save them for you for breakfast." Hudson handed his mother the bag of mangoes.

"My favorite!" she practically squealed with delight. She pulled Hudson close for a hug and then ruffled his hair. "Get ready for bed, beta. And make sure you wash your hair."

Five

Hudson woke up early the next morning to the loud hum of the blender. He rolled over and looked at the clock. It was seven a.m. He had slept only a few hours, alternating between good dreams about all the lovely things he would like to bake if he did enter the cupcake competition and nightmares about missing an *Our Time* performance because he was too busy baking.

After a few minutes, Hudson finally got out of bed and wandered into the kitchen. He found his grandmother pouring herself a glass of freshly made lassi from the blender.

"Oh! Good morning, Nani. I didn't expect to find you here," he said, greeting his grandmother. She had come to live with Hudson's family shortly before *Our Time* opened, when her husband had passed away. Although she had lived in India most of her life, she had adjusted well to being in the United States and had made friends with other widows in the community. Hudson had met her only once, in India, when he was very young, and he was hoping to get to know her better, but she was hardly ever home.

"Good morning, Harshdev!" his nani chirped. She didn't notice Hudson wince at her use of his Gujarati name. "Would you like some lassi? I found these beautiful mangoes in the kitchen this morning. It's been so long since I had homemade lassi."

"Wait—those are the mangoes I bought for Mom," Hudson said, a little annoyed. "I was going to cut them up for her for breakfast. I know they're her favorite."

"Oh, Hudson, don't you worry. I think she will still be very happy. Your mother loved mango lassi growing up back in India. She probably hasn't had really good lassi in a long time. And trust me: this is very good lassi."

Hudson giggled at his nani's self-confidence. He had tasted lassi before, but he was not a big fan. The yogurt-based drink was very filling. But he thought it would be rude to say no. "Okay," he said. "I'll have a small glass."

"Ah, nahee, there is no 'small glass' when you have lassi," his nani insisted. She found a large one in the cupboard and filled it up to the top. "Here you go. Drink up!"

Hudson tentatively took a sip. He was impressed. The texture of this lassi was great—not too thick and more like a smoothie than he remembered. And the addition of cardamom was excellent. But there was something else in there—something Hudson couldn't quite place.

"Ah, you taste something special, don't you?" Hudson's nani was watching him closely. She had a twinkle in her eye and a playful grin on her face.

Hudson nodded eagerly before taking another sip. "What is it? It's spicy—"

"Ah, I cannot share my secret!" His nani cut him off quickly. She glanced at the clock on the microwave. "Oh dear! I have to go. Please make sure your mother gets some lassi when she wakes up. I think she will be nicely surprised. I'll leave the rest in the fridge."

"But where are you going?" Hudson asked, now sad that his nani was leaving.

She smiled again. "I'm going to teach my friends chess!" she said. "I haven't played in years. Your grandfather taught me long ago, and we always enjoyed it. We stopped playing when he became ill." She looked away, wiping a tear from her eye. But she soon smiled again. "I've put on one of my favorite kurtas for the occasion! Do you like it?" She twirled for her grandson, showing off her elderberry-blue kurta, a long shirt. It was embroidered with silver stars, making it shimmer like a night sky. She had paired it with loose matching pants.

"It's absolutely beautiful," Hudson agreed.

"Thank you! I made it myself years ago, and I'm amazed it still fits. But I have to run now!" A moment later, she was out the door.

Hudson took another sip of his mango lassi. "What is that?" he muttered aloud. "Paprika?"

He was still mulling over the mystery spice while he flipped on FoodTube. Almost immediately, the ad for the cupcake competition came on. There was Charlie Richards in his cowboy getup, encouraging talented young bakers to enter.

I guess it couldn't hurt, Hudson thought.

And like that, he was in action. He looked in the fridge for ingredients, ready to run to the store if necessary. But he was in luck: everything he needed to make raspberry Linzer cookies was there in the house. Before getting started, though, he made sure to set up his camera, just as he would when filming his own FoodTube show.

"It's just like an episode of *Broadway Sizzlers*," Hudson said, giving himself a pep talk. He very rarely shot an episode without a celebrity guest. "I may be by myself, but I can do this. Channel your inner Ethel Merman—be poised and elegant." He took a deep breath and pressed record.

"Hi!" he said to the camera. "I'm Hudson Patel. I'm thirteen years old, and I live in Manhattan. I enjoy cooking, but I really love baking. . . ." He suddenly felt a lump in his throat as the memory of the messy attempt at making a Baked Alaska came back to him. But then he recalled how his mother had actually eaten it and seemed to enjoy it. He pressed on. "For my entry submission to the Bake It Till You Make It competition, I'm making raspberry Linzer cookies. These are very popular during the holidays, but I like to think that every day is a holiday!" Hudson swung into high gear. He was in his element, bringing his Broadway charisma to the video.

Hudson worked away, and when the cookies were complete, he uploaded the video to the competition website.

"Here goes nothing," he said. Then he pressed submit.

Later, when Hudson arrived at the Ethel Merman, Relly, Monica, and April were nowhere to be found. "They're all in the basement," Jimmy Onions said.

The basement meant homework—so the Squad avoided it as much as possible. Hudson walked into the dressing room he shared with Relly and set the box of raspberry Linzer cookies on the counter. After making them that morning and submitting his official entry video, he was already tired—and nervous. He hoped, though, that his friends would appreciate the effort and accept the cookies as an apology for leaving them abruptly the previous night.

Hudson was putting on his costume when Relly walked into their dressing room. "Hi," Hudson said, trying his best to sound cheerful and apologetic all at once. "I brought cookies today."

Relly could never resist Hudson's cookies. He rubbed his hands together eagerly as he eyed the box. "What kind do we have here?" he said. Monica and April poked their heads through the open door.

"They're April's favorite flavor—raspberry," Hudson said. April bounced in excitement. Seeing her friends making up, Monica smiled too.

"I'm sorry about last night," Hudson said.

"A lot happened all at once," Monica said as she stepped into the room. "We were all pretty stunned by the news."

"I know how much you love baking and cooking, Hudson, but the news about *Move It!* was really big!" April exclaimed as she took a picture of the cookies on her phone. *#BroadwayFuel.* "And that whole episode with Tabitha was just so upsetting. She was particularly mean to you!"

"Well, Tabitha was right, wasn't she?" Hudson said.

He avoided his friends' eyes. "I'm not the strongest singer, dancer, or actor. I just feel really lucky to be here. It took me years to get cast in an off-Broadway show, and now I'm starring in *Our Time*. This could be the highlight of my Broadway career! From diaper commercials to Broadway—that's a pretty good run, don't you think?"

"How can you say that?" April squawked between bites of cookie. "Don't you want a long Broadway career?"

"I'd love that as much as you would," Hudson said. "But I really think I got lucky with *Our Time*.'"

"So you don't really care if you're here with us or not?" Relly asked quizzically. "Is that why this cupcake competition means so much?"

"It means so much because I love to bake. It's a huge opportunity. That *People* article that came out a few months ago helped boost *Our Time*, but it also got me lots of followers for FoodTube and on my own social media channels." He noticed the concerned looks on his friends' faces. "But don't worry," he continued confidently. "I'm not leaving this show unless I'm forced out. And I'm not going to win the cupcake competition."

"What?!" his friends all said at once.

Just then Claudia interrupted them. "What's this 'What?'" she said. "That's no way to warm up! Come on, it's time to get ready for the show!"

Claudia shuffled the four friends out of the dressing room and had them start through their scales and stretches. It was another good night, with a sold-out crowd.

"Maybe we don't really need to worry about *Move It!*," Relly said as the after-show crowd dispersed when they finished signing autographs.

But April set him straight. "We can't rest!" she exclaimed. "New show, new kids, new competition. And *Tabitha*."

"Okay, then. I stand corrected." Relly widened his eyes at Hudson. The Squad was exhausted after another long week of shows, and the drama about *Move It!* had left them all more tired than usual. They got a quick pizza dinner and headed home.

But a few days later, after a great show with a very enthusiastic audience, April gathered the Squad backstage.

"Okay, all, we are going to go have a nice post-show get-together. We deserve it after our performance tonight!"

The four friends considered going to Al Joseph's, one of their favorite restaurants, but instead, they decided to venture farther south in Manhattan. They took a short subway ride to Nolita and settled in at Nom Wah Tea Parlor. On the way over, they had agreed not to speak of *Move It!* or Tabitha. It was too stressful.

The Squad entered the small restaurant. They claimed a table for themselves and pulled up the menu.

"Ooh, we totally need to get the fried dim sum sampler platter!" April exclaimed.

"So, what's up with the cupcake competition?" Monica asked Hudson once they'd put in their order. "What have you found out?"

Hudson stared at the menu, continuing to look it over even though the food was already on its way. He struggled with what to tell his friends. Finally, he simply said, "Well, I entered. Remember those raspberry Linzer cookies?"

"Ah, dreamy," April said. "I love raspberries."

"Those were really good," Relly said, rubbing his belly.

"They were," Monica agreed. "But what about them?"

"That was my submission for the competition. I made a video of myself making them. I was more nervous filming it than I was for my *Our Time* audition!"

April let out a long chuckle. "Mr. *Broadway Sizzlers* had trouble filming a video of himself baking?"

"I was just getting camera shy. Usually I have a guest, but this time I was all alone. I fumbled over the dough a bit, but I didn't really have time to redo the recipe. So, hopefully it went okay."

"How did you ever get through an audition?" April asked.

"Luck."

Hudson paused to take a sip of water before continuing. "Also, Charlie Richards said there's going to be a twist on the real competition. The finalists will have to make up their own recipes within some sort of rules that haven't been revealed yet. But I'm not that creative with my baking—I'm used to making other people's recipes."

"It will be fine, Hudson," Monica said. "You're more creative than you think."

"Send us a copy of your submission video," April added. "I want to see what goes into making the stuff you feed us every night." She pulled out her phone, but the color suddenly drained from her face.

"What's wrong?" Hudson said.

April couldn't speak, let alone breathe. "It's . . . it's . . . it's Tabitha and *Move It!* All over again!"

"We weren't going to talk about that," Relly said quietly, just as their sodas arrived.

"But Tabitha's going to be a kids cohost for the Fall Festival in Duffy Square next month! We're performing with a bunch of other big shows, and now *Move It!* is going to be showcased as a 'hot new show opening soon!'"

April continued reading from her phone.

"There's also more information about the show itself. It's *interactive!* Tabitha makes her entrance on a crystal ball; there is fog and water squirting at the seats and even small pyrotechnics for the finale." April threw her phone down onto the cushioned seat next to her. "WHAT ARE WE GOING TO DO?!"

Monica, Relly, and Hudson weren't quite sure how to respond. "Well, there's not a lot we can do at this very moment," Monica whispered. Right then the server came over with the food.

"So, let's eat," Relly suggested. Surprisingly, April was quiet and picked up her chopsticks. She expertly dug into the fifty-piece spread, starting with a spring roll, while Hudson and Relly went directly for the fried shrimp balls. Monica tried a pan-fried dumpling.

The famished friends ate quietly, savoring the mix of flavors and the textures of the various types of dim sum. They all enjoyed the distraction from any more *Move It!* news.

"I love dim sum," Relly said.

"Me too. But I hate *Move It!*" April was nearly shouting again.

"How about we head over to Little Italy for some dessert? I could go for a cannoli," suggested Monica. "Hudson, have you ever made cannoli?" She was clearly trying to steer the conversation back to the cupcake competition.

"No, I haven't," he said. "But that would have been an excellent submission for the cupcake competition."

The Squad split the bill and gathered up their belongings before starting the short walk to Ferrara Bakery, a beloved institution in Little Italy.

The four friends gathered around the bakery case to look at the wide selection of sweets. Even April, upset as she was, couldn't help but grin at the offerings: not just cannoli but éclairs, tiramisu, rainbow cookies, New York cheesecake. It was all so tantalizing. April snapped a picture. *#DessertHeaven*

Monica ordered a chocolate cannoli, Hudson opted for a slice of chocolate truffle cake, and April chose a sfogliatella, a flaky pastry filled with ricotta and candied fruit. She even pronounced it perfectly, impressing not only her friends but also the bakery staff. After much consideration, Relly settled on an Isabelle, one of the bakery's specials: a base of chocolate cake with chocolate mousse, raspberry jam, and chocolate ganache.

"That's a lot of . . . chocolate," Monica said, impressed.

"I've never had it before," Relly admitted. "But I think my sweet tooth can handle it." He smiled wide.

The Squad settled in at their table. A gasp from Hudson snapped Monica, Relly, and April to attention.

"What? What happened? What have those *Move It!* people done now?" April demanded.

Monica studied Hudson's face closely for a moment while he continued to read something on his phone. "I don't think this is about *Move It!*, April," she whispered.

The Squad's desserts arrived, and Relly, April, and Monica dug into theirs while Hudson continued to stare at the message on his phone.

"Well, what is it?" April insisted, wiping pastry flakes from her mouth.

Hudson blew the hair out of his eyes and then finally looked up at his friends. He took a deep breath. "It's about the cupcake competition," he said. "The subject line just says 'Congrats!' Inside it says, 'You're a finalist for Bake It Till You Make It!' Then there's a link to a video."

"So watch it!" April said, reaching across the table to grab Hudson's phone, but he pulled it away just in time to avoid her.

"Let him do it, April," Monica chided her friend gently. "Whenever you're ready, Hudson." She couldn't help herself and added, "This is so exciting!"

Hudson gave Monica a meek smile and hesitated a few moments longer before he finally pressed play.

Charlie Richards's voice flooded their corner of the bakery. He was standing in front of a blank wall. Unlike the elaborate, professional productions his FoodTube show usually had, this video looked like he had shot it himself at home.

"Howdy, Hudson!" Charlie said. "A big congratulations

to you! You're a finalist in Bake It Till You Make It! Your raspberry Linzer cookies were really impressive, and I have to say, I'd love to try one. The technique you demonstrated and your care for the process really caught my eye, and I think you have a lot to offer in this competition.

"I come from a ranching family. My grandfather had a restaurant in Colorado, where he served farm-to-table food. He taught his customers to appreciate and respect plants and animals. It was my family that got me interested in food—and how I ultimately fell in love with learning about people and cuisines from all over the world. So, for the competition, I want you to use flavors from your family background to make something unique. Don't use preexisting recipes that anyone can find online—or on FoodTube.

"On the day of the competition, you may bring your own ingredients. We'll provide staples like milk, eggs, and flour, as well as the tools like spatulas, cupcake pans, mixers—and of course the ovens and stoves. Just submit a list of the ingredients the morning of the competition. You are welcome to bring family and friends to be in the audience, but send us their names in advance.

"Remember: the winner gets a kiosk to sell their creation in the middle of Times Square for the summer. Be creative, and have fun whipping up your cupcake creation! Till next time." Charlie tipped his cowboy hat at the camera, the fringe of his jacket swinging and casting shadows on the wall behind him.

"Eeeeek, this is so exciting!" Monica squealed. "Hudson, you have a shot at selling your creation to hundreds—no, thousands—of people!"

April snapped a picture of Hudson. She was about to upload it with *#BakeItTillYouMakeItFinalist!*, when she realized Hudson didn't seem too happy about the news. Relly reached out for a high five, but Hudson had slumped back in his chair and closed his eyes, his hands hidden in the pockets of his blue windbreaker. He hadn't even touched his chocolate truffle cake.

"What's up, Hudson?" Relly asked gently, using a napkin to clean off chocolate that had fallen on his shirt.

Hudson simply shook his head.

"Hudson, you have to explain yourself," April said gently. "Isn't this good news?"

Finally, Hudson opened his eyes. His friends thought he might cry.

"I'm not qualified," he said simply and matter-of-factly.

"You? Not qualified?" Relly said, his voice so loud that other diners turned to look in the Squad's direction. "How could you, Hudson Patel, star of his own FoodTube show *Broadway Sizzlers*, with guests like Selena Gomez, not be qualified for this cupcake competition?"

"Yeah, Hudson, tell us. How could you not be qualified?"

Hudson looked at each of his friends. "You heard Charlie: The finalists will have to use family recipes and touches from their ethnic background cuisine. I don't know anything about Indian culture or Indian food. And I certainly don't know anything about 'family flavors.' So I'm not qualified."

And once again, he got up to leave. "I really want to be alone right now," he said. "I'll see you all at the theater."

Six

"Hudson, you have to stop leaving us all so suddenly," Relly scolded his friend at the theater the next day.

The Squad was sitting in a corner of the main theater, sprawled out on the audience chairs. They were snacking away on popcorn and drinking bubble tea that Monica had picked up on her way in. Jimmy, who seemed to never leave the Ethel Merman, had let them in early so they could talk. Text messages had flown from phone to phone all night.

Hudson, where are you? Monica had wanted to know. **We're concerned.**

You have to talk to us, April wrote. **We want to help. Oh, and we have to talk about "Move It!"**

Stop with Move It! for a bit, April. Let's focus on one crisis at a time, Relly had written.

Finally, when Hudson failed to respond, Monica had suggested a meeting at the Ethel Merman.

Hudson had been the last to arrive, and when he did, he was empty-handed—no conciliatory treats for his friends this time. Monica, April, and Relly knew better than to say anything about it.

"Before we start this intervention," April began, "I want you all to know that I've decided to invest more in TikTok."

"Sounds like we need yet another intervention," Relly said. "Too many social media platforms to keep up with. I was just getting the hang of Instagram."

"Well, Relly," April retorted, "if we're going to stay ahead of *Move It!*, we have to make sure we have as great a reach and as big an audience as possible. So, I'm focusing on TikTok now. I'm doing all the TikTok dance challenges and trying to come up with some of my own. We should all be doing it. And when we become the biggest thing on TikTok, Broadway won't forget us."

"Broadway *can't* forget us, April." Relly was clearly annoyed. "We've still got sold-out crowds every night, and we've got lines of people wanting our autographs after the show. *Every* show."

"I don't mind doing a few TikTok dances," Monica said.

"It could be fun." She looked around the theater. "I really love this place," she continued. "But a little creativity on the side couldn't hurt us. It could even help us stay on our game."

"Okay, fine, so we'll do some TikTok videos," Relly said. "But can we please talk about why Hudson is being so down on himself? I feel like I'm losing my friend."

Hudson finally looked up. He could tell how much Relly, Monica, and April cared. It was time to open up to the Squad.

"I can't go forward with the cupcake competition, and I'm really bummed about it," Hudson began. "Like I said last night, I'm not qualified. I don't know anything about Indian cooking, so how am I supposed to follow the rules of the competition?"

He scarfed down a handful of popcorn before continuing.

"I really like my mom's food, but she makes up her own recipes a lot. I think it's a creative outlet for her after being in the hospital all day. And when my dad cooks—well, he keeps it simple, like baked salmon and broccoli. He says it helps him stay healthy."

"Do you speak the Indian language?" Monica asked.

"There are a lot of them," Hudson said. "I understand my parents when they speak in Hindi, but I can hardly say a full sentence back to them. And Gujarati, their native language, is a mystery to me. I think I picked up Hindi better because we watched a lot of Bollywood movies when I was a kid. Apparently, I liked to dance to Priyanka Chopra movies when I was really young."

"She makes Indian movies too?" April said, amazed. "Talk about a real megastar!"

"Yeah, you should see *Bajirao Mastani*. Priyanka's done it all, it seems," Hudson said. "I wish I could too."

"What, you want to star in Bollywood movies?" Relly asked. "They are pretty fun, from what I've heard. Always some sort of song and dance." His face lit up as he thought of all the new moves he could learn from Indian movies.

"That's not what I meant," Hudson said. "I wish I had room for both Broadway and baking, but it all feels like too much."

Monica handed Hudson his bubble tea.

"Have you ever been to India?" she asked.

"I was born there, but we moved to New York when I was really young. We went back once, but I don't remember it. We don't really have a lot of family there anymore, especially now that my grandfather passed away and my grandmother lives here with us."

"What about cousins, aunts, and uncles? Extended family?" Monica asked.

"My dad has a sister there. She brought my cousins

to see the opening of *Our Time*." Hudson paused to think, resting his chin on the palm of his right hand. "No one besides that," he finally said. "I think most of my extended family is in England now or scattered across the US. And one of my cousins lives in New Zealand."

"Ooooohhhh, New Zealand! I want to go there! They have more sheep than people!" April exclaimed.

"That's a very random fact." Monica giggled. "But what about your grandmother? And your parents? What can they tell you about India?"

"You must still watch those Bollywood movies," Relly interjected.

"It's been a while, but sometimes, yes, I watch a Bollywood movie with my family. I'm usually at the theater, though, or baking or doing homework—we should really be doing homework, shouldn't we?" Hudson cringed as he thought about all the homework he had to catch up on.

"This is far more interesting," Relly said.

"What about holidays?" Monica tried very hard to keep the conversation on track. "Do you celebrate traditional Indian holidays at all?"

Suddenly Hudson sat up in his chair and started scrolling through the calendar on his phone. "You know, Monica," he said, "I'm really glad you asked that. We have a big holiday coming up. Yeah, here it is. In just a few days—Diwali!"

"What's Di-wa-li?" Monica sounded out the syllables carefully. Hudson handed her his phone so she could see pictures he had pulled up on Pinterest. "And what are all these candles?" Monica's face lit up. She was enthralled with the colors and lights.

"Those are diyas. They're oil lamps that we light for good luck. Diwali is a huge festival, probably the biggest one we have. It's the Festival of Lights, when we celebrate good winning over evil." Hudson was suddenly more animated and excited than his friends had seen him in days. "It's my grandmother's favorite holiday—after Valentine's Day." He chuckled. "Even though my grandfather is gone, she loves all the flowers and heart-shaped chocolate boxes." The four friends laughed, all thinking about their own grandparents.

"Oh, good, you're all here!" The Squad turned toward a man dressed in a bright papaya-colored suit. As soon as they spotted the cotton-candy-pink lenses in the thick plum frames and the giant yellow sunflower bobbing in his breast pocket, the Squad knew who this man was: Rick Gallo, *Our Time*'s producer. His quirky and colorful outfits were the source of his nickname: Slick Rick.

"Oh no," April hissed. "What's *he* doing here? The producer never comes to the show unless something's *wrong!*"

At Rick's heels was Artie, who was followed closely by

Claudia. Slick Rick climbed the steps to the stage and spun around to face Artie. "Call everyone out here!" He twirled his index finger in the air, as if to summon the cast and crew by magic.

The entire cast and crew soon crowded the stage. They all shrank at the sight of Rick, who paired his bright suit with a lemon-yellow shirt and a blueberry-colored tie. This producer was a star in his own right. He and Artie had a long history of hits, and they were often spotted at the swanky Calf Club, having long lunches in the luxurious red booths.

"All right, everyone!" Rick bellowed. "We've got to get it together. *You've* got to get it together. I've put a lot of money into this show, and by a stroke of luck"—here he grinned at Monica, who blushed—"it's been a huge success. Even *my* Instagram followers have shot through the roof." Now he fist-bumped April. "We've got talent here"—Rick shuffled his feet before Relly—"but we're seeing our numbers slip a bit." He paused before Hudson. "We've had some stumbling in the last few shows, and I want to smooth everything out before the Fall Festival and before *Move It!* opens. We've got to keep my star—I mean *our* star—shining bright!"

By now everyone's eyes had settled on Hudson, who desperately wished a trapdoor would open beneath him and release him into the belly of the theater.

"Yes, we've got to stay on our game. No, we've got to step it up!" This time it was Artie. He adjusted his scarf as he stepped forward into the center of the circle to join Rick. "So, I've called back Maria Marquez to help with our choreography and Mr. Fernando to make sure our singing is pitch perfect."

Hudson let out a low groan. As much as he liked Maria and Mr. Fernando, he hated working with them. He knew—everyone knew—he was the weakest singer and dancer in the show, and having the experts back meant lots of work.

The rest of the cast left the stage, leaving the Squad to rehearse.

"It's going to be okay, Hudson," Monica said. She gave her friend a hug, but she could tell he was upset.

"This is another part of my problem," Hudson said. "I love baking so much, and I also love performing, but I don't really feel at home anywhere."

"But, Hudson, you're on *Broadway*!" April exclaimed. "Do you know how lucky you are? How lucky we *all are*? Yeah, I know I've been a little obsessed with *Move It!* And, yeah, that show will be competition for us—and we have to work really hard to make sure we don't lose our title as cutest, most lovable on Broadway. But we're a team, and we'll make it happen!" With that, April stomped her foot and crossed to the far end of the stage, where Maria and Mr. Fernando were waiting.

Monica, Hudson, and Relly were stunned by April's enthusiasm.

"We should have put that on social media," Monica said, making Hudson and Relly laugh.

Under Maria's direction, the Squad spent the next hour going over the living room scene that opened *Our Time*. Then they spent an hour practicing the most difficult songs in the show. By the time they finished, the entire Squad, including Hudson, was feeling energized and upbeat. They hadn't felt that prepared in a long time.

"This is going to be our best show yet!" Relly pumped his fist in the air.

"Ooohhh, maybe we should put something on TikTok! Our first TikTok together!" April said.

"What will we say?" Relly asked.

"What you just said," April said. "Show confidence and enthusiasm. We want to intimidate the competition without being overly forceful."

"It looks like April may have a directing career in her future, you know, once she's mastered this whole being-a-star-on-Broadway thing," Hudson whispered to Monica. April got Relly into just the right light and then pulled Monica and Hudson into the frame behind him.

"Okay! Three, two, one, *ACTION!*"

"Hey there, fans of *Our Time!*" Relly was quite suave. It was clear he was made for the spotlight. "We've been working all afternoon to perfect our smooth moves so we can bring you the best show yet! We hope to see you on Broadway soon!"

He broke into a slide and moved out of frame. Hudson waved at the camera, and Monica curtsied.

"Perfect!" April said. "We're going to rock it tonight!" She did a pirouette as she posted the video.

The show was practically seamless, the best in weeks. It was just the confidence the Squad—and the rest of the cast and crew—needed.

"Who wants to celebrate a great show?" April asked as she and the others collected their belongings after signing autographs.

"I should really get home," Hudson said. "I've been out late a lot recently, and I'm beat. And I have to catch up on homework. And withdraw from the cupcake competition."

"But you were so excited about Diwali!" Monica stepped in front of her friend. She was clearly no longer the shy young girl who had come from California just a year before. But then she furrowed her brow. "Did I say it right?"

"Yes, you said it just fine, Monica," Hudson reassured his friend. He appreciated her support. The four friends started walking toward the back exit of the Ethel Merman. Relly and April were in front, eagerly coming up with ideas for more TikTok videos. Hudson and Monica lagged behind.

"Well, if you're excited about Diwali, I think you can get excited about the competition. Think about how you can learn something new. Remember all those cookie recipes from my abuelita that you mastered?" Hudson shrugged. Monica continued. "It's not necessarily about winning. It's about the experience and the attempt. You know, there's no reason for me to be here on Broadway. But here I am! Even if you don't win, it'll be a cool experience."

Jimmy Onions was holding the door open for them. "April and Relly said you're heading home, Hudson. No pizza or fancy feasts tonight?"

"Not tonight, Jimmy. I've got too much to do," Hudson said.

"Well, Hudson, you know what they say: 'There's no place like home.'" He threw a handful of popcorn into his mouth and winked, disappearing into the dark hallway of the theater as the door shut behind him.

Seven

Despite being tired and needing to catch up on homework, Hudson decided to walk back to the Upper West Side. This time he didn't stop at Fairway or anywhere else. He was absorbed in his thoughts, certain he wouldn't win the cupcake competition. The humiliation of defeat would be too much to bear. But Monica's words kept ringing in his ears. He had to take a chance. He wouldn't know unless he tried, right?

Before he knew it, Hudson was outside the building where his family lived. He hesitated before climbing the steps to his home and going inside. It wasn't too late, but it was late enough, and he was always afraid he would wake his family.

When he opened the front door, he was still amazed that it didn't squeak. But he was even more amazed to find his mom sitting at the counter again. This time she was reading a magazine and snacking on a leftover raspberry Linzer cookie.

"Where did you get that?" Hudson asked. "I thought I took all of them to the theater days ago."

Crumbs and powdered sugar covered his mother's mouth. She stared at Hudson for a moment. "I kept a few aside. For a treat."

Hudson grinned. He knew his mother had a sweet tooth, but he also knew she did her best to control it. He was flattered that she was hiding his creations to enjoy on her own time.

"But tell me, Hudson," she said, looking her son over carefully after he untied his white sneakers and set them aside by the door. "Why do you look so glum?"

"What do you mean?" Hudson was trying his best to be cheerful. He turned away to hang up his backpack and jacket.

His mom slid off the stool and walked over to the sink to wash away the powdered sugar from her hands.

"Something's on your mind," she said, approaching her son.

This time Hudson put both his hands in his hair and then massaged his hairline with his fingertips.

"Well?" his mother said.

"I made it to the final round of the cupcake competition," he blurted out. "I'm a finalist."

"That's so exciting, Hudson! I'm very proud of you!" Hudson's mom tried to throw her arms around him for a hug.

Before she could, though, Hudson quickly added, "I'm thinking about dropping out."

His mother dropped her arms and narrowed her eyes at her son. "And why would you do that?"

Hudson could tell he was in for a battle. But he gave his mother the same answer he had given his friends. "I'm not qualified."

Hudson expected his mother to get upset—to raise her voice and send him to his room. Instead, she chuckled.

"I don't get it. What's so funny?"

"*You* are, my son," she said. "How could you not be qualified?"

"Well," Hudson sighed. "I have to come up with a recipe of my own—something unique. I don't know how to do that."

Hudson's mother laughed again. "Hudson, you are always experimenting in the kitchen. You're always cutting it *so close* in getting to the theater, and you're often behind on your homework." She paused and tilted her head. Hudson could tell she knew that he was, in fact, terribly behind on his homework. "Why? So you can make new things in the kitchen. You know so much about how different flavors work together. What's stopping you from making something new now?"

She leaned back against the kitchen counter. Hudson sat down on the stool she had vacated. He knew he had to tell his mother the final twist on the competition rules.

"All the finalists have to use flavors from their family cuisines," Hudson explained. "So for me, that would be flavors from India. And you know I've never cooked Indian food."

Now Hudson's mother was very serious. "Hudson, you have no idea that you've got the perfect person to help you."

"Who? You?" he asked.

"No. But close. Your nani."

"My nani?" Hudson was confused. "But she's hardly ever here. You and Dad do most of the cooking."

Somehow, this was funny, as Hudson's mother began to laugh again.

"You mastered her pralines, remember?"

"But those weren't her recipe. They were a recipe three generations old!"

"Hudson, where do you think I learned to cook? From my mother. She taught me everything I know." Hudson's mom seemed wistful for a moment. "But I was very focused on getting through school, so I didn't learn it well." She looked at Hudson again. "It's important to have a lot of different interests, to nurture them," she said. "It keeps life fun and engaging."

Now it was Hudson's turn to reflect. "Is that why you let me spend all this time with both theater and baking?" he asked.

"Beta, you're very talented. And you like those activities. You should pursue them so long as you find them fun, interesting, and challenging. That's the key here. The cupcake competition is a new challenge. And your grandmother can help you." She walked to the sink and washed her hands. "By the way, are you hungry?"

Hudson realized he was indeed very hungry. "Would you like some homemade samosas? Guess who made them?" She winked at Hudson, as she turned off the faucet. She walked over to the far counter and uncovered a tray of the triangular pastries stuffed with potatoes, peas, and spices.

"Nani made these?" Hudson was impressed. He had only had samosas from restaurants, never homemade ones.

"She did," his mother said. "It's her own special recipe. She made golgappas, too, this afternoon, but your father and I ate them all. Well, your father ate most of them. They're his favorite, you know."

"Wow," Hudson said, taking a big bite of a samosa. These ones were crispy, and the pastry shell was more delicate than the ones he'd had in restaurants. "These are very good. That's a great mix of spices." He thought for a moment, racking his brain as he tasted a familiar spice.

"There's something interesting here," Hudson said. Suddenly it hit him. "It's the same thing she put in the mango lassi!"

Once again Hudson's mother laughed, gently this time. "Your nani will never reveal that secret," she said. "She picked up tricks throughout her travels with my father over the years, and that's one she will never tell me—what's in that mango lassi. And now you're telling me you taste it in the samosa!"

"I do! But I can't tell what it is. It could be paprika, but I don't think it is." He took another bite and then shook his head. "Where could she have picked that up?" he asked aloud, but not really expecting an answer.

"Do you know her story? My parents' story?" Hudson's mother asked. "I'm not sure I've ever really told you."

"I know that she lived in Goa with my grandfather before he passed away," Hudson said hesitantly. "But when we visited India when I was very young, weren't they living somewhere else?"

"They were," Hudson's mother said. "But let me start

from the beginning." Hudson's mother picked up a samosa from the platter. She sat on another stool next to her son, took a small bite, closing her eyes to savor the flavors, and then began.

"Your grandmother was a very talented dancer. Come to think of it, that's probably where you got your flair for theater and dance," she added, nudging Hudson in the arm with her elbow. "Everyone knows your father and I both have two left feet." They laughed. It was true—his mother was shy about dancing, and although his father tried, he really only had one move: hands in fists above his head while he stepped side to side.

"I think I inherited that, too," Hudson said.

Hudson's mother ignored his comment. "Your nani wanted to become a professional dancer, and she learned all the dances of India, from bharata natyam to bhangra. When she and my father met and married, they left Gujarat so my father could go to medical school in England. Your uncle was born about two years after they arrived in England, and I was born three years after that. Your aunt was born two years after me. So my mother was busy raising children and running the household in a foreign land.

"It was then that she invested in perfecting her cooking skills. She was a master of Indian cuisine but also picked up new ones as they traveled. She can cook anything,

Hudson. *Anything at all.* And she's made up her own recipes too. She'll take simple ingredients and make them into something phenomenal."

"That's so cool!" Hudson was truly dazzled. "But what about the dancing? Did she just stop?"

"Well, later my parents returned to India so that my father could teach at a medical school east of Mumbai. My mother was still too busy to dance full-time. But she would dance with us kids at home. And at parties." Hudson's mom smiled at the memories. "You should have seen her. Everyone's eyes would be on her as she floated across the dance floor. She was quite a sight to see. I tried to dance like her, but I could never be as good."

"Wait." Hudson stopped his mother mid-story. "You? Dance? You always refuse to dance. You're shy! And you just said you have two left feet!"

"Well, it's my turn to confess," she said, looking nostalgic. "I loved to dance, and my parents both encouraged me. But when I got really busy with my medical studies, I felt I had to choose. And when I set my sights on an oncology career, I really buckled down. I thought there wasn't any more time for a fun hobby like dancing. But I do really love to dance."

"And she was a wonderful dancer, beta." The voice startled both Hudson and his mother. They looked up to find

Hudson's nani standing just inside the front door. She was wearing a bright persimmon-colored shawl. A chestnut handbag was draped across her body.

"Mom!" Hudson's mother said. "Where are you going? It's so late!"

"I'm not going. I've just come home," she said. "You know, this door no longer squeaks." She winked at her daughter and grandson. It was the same wink Hudson's mom would give him.

"Where have you been, Nani?" Hudson wondered.

"You won't believe it, but I've been out dancing!"

"What?" Hudson and his mother exclaimed at the same time.

Nani let out a jolly laugh. "Well, it started out as another chess lesson, but then my friend Mrs. Barton decided we should go to a salsa lesson. We had seen some dancers in Central Park recently, and she said she had always wanted to salsa. So, we looked on her phone and found a place that had a lesson tonight. And we went." She giggled again.

Hudson's mother laughed too. "Did you have a good time?" she asked.

Nani nodded. "I did. I had a fabulous time! Next time you should both come with me." She spotted the platter of samosas on the table. "Oh! Are you enjoying my samosas? It's been so long since I made them. I hope they turned out okay."

"They're delicious," Hudson said. "But there's a spice in there that I can't quite put my finger on. Like the lassi."

"Oh, that's my secret," his nani said. "Maybe one day I'll share it with you—but not yet." She winked again as she hung up her handbag and loosened her shawl.

"Hudson has some big news," his mother announced.

"I do?" Hudson was confused.

"Oh really?" his nani said. "That's exciting! I love news, especially when it concerns my very talented grandchildren." She clapped her hands together lightly. "What have you accomplished? What are we to celebrate?"

"I'm not sure . . . " Hudson hesitated.

"The cupcake competition, Hudson," his mother whispered, leaning close to her son and nudging him with her elbow again. "Tell her about the competition."

"Cupcake competition?" his nani asked. "I certainly love cupcakes. Have you won a cupcake competition?"

"No," Hudson said. "I'm a finalist." He looked at his mother imploringly.

"A finalist! In a cupcake competition!" Nani was beaming. "That's so wonderful!"

"Talk to your grandmother," his mother whispered. She ruffled his hair before walking out of the kitchen toward her bedroom, leaving Hudson and his nani to talk.

Eight

Now Hudson was alone with his nani. He suddenly became nervous, watching her carefully. She had traded her stylish shoes for a pair of fuzzy slippers. She glided over to a cabinet and retrieved a small plate.

"It's just big enough for one samosa. Otherwise I'll eat too many." She giggled again.

Hudson smiled back. He had never realized just how jolly his grandmother was. Or how light on her feet. She was practically dancing now as she moved around the kitchen, first picking up a samosa from the platter, then turning to the sink for a paper towel to cover the plate, and finally to the microwave, where she would warm the samosa (but "just a pinch"). Hudson found himself awkwardly shuffling around her to stay out of her way. Ultimately, he bumped into a far counter, knocking over a bowl of oranges that was precariously close to the edge. Somehow, Hudson's nani caught the bowl—one that she had brought with her from India—before Hudson even realized what was happening.

"Sorry," he muttered as he bent over to pick up the oranges. They were just getting ripe, and their fragrance was still more tart than sweet.

"No need to apologize, beta," his nani said, smiling at her grandson as he gathered up the oranges. "You know, this bowl has traveled very far and very long," she said. She didn't say anything more for several moments; she simply ran her fingertips along the bowl's polished edge. Then she suddenly flipped the bowl over and read the inscription on the back. "Kampala, Uganda, 1985." She was quiet again for a moment and then looked back up at Hudson. "You know, your grandfather and I lived there for several months. He took on a medical assignment so we could see something new."

"Wow," Hudson said again. "I didn't know you traveled that far."

"Oh, your grandfather and I traveled very far and wide over the years, especially after your mother and her siblings were grown and gone. We saw Thailand, Malaysia, the

Galapagos Islands, Machu Picchu." Hudson's nani got very quiet and looked down at her feet. Then she said softly, "Our last trip together was to Japan. We knew your grandfather was ill by that time, but he had always wanted to see Japan, so we booked that last trip. He passed away three years later."

Hudson stepped closer to his grandmother and put his hand on her shoulder. He gave it a small squeeze, but she swallowed him in a big hug.

"You would have liked your grandfather very much," she said, letting Hudson go. "He was quiet on the surface, but he had a mischievous side. He was always telling silly jokes. I must have heard the same ones hundreds—if not thousands—of times over the years."

"Sounds like my dad," Hudson said, rolling his eyes.

"Absolutely!" his grandmother said, taking the samosa out of the microwave. She took a nibble and then scrunched her nose and puckered her lips. When she squeezed her eyes shut tight, Hudson knew what she was doing.

"What's missing, Nani?" he asked.

"Lime!" she exclaimed. "Oh, I let out one of my secrets!" She slammed her wrist on the counter playfully as she took another bite. "Yes, lime would have added more punch. Some would have said cilantro, but I have always hated cilantro."

"Me too!" Hudson said. "It tastes like soap."

"Yes, it does. And my own mother used to put it in everything. Lots of it. I hated it." She took two more samosas from the tray and placed one on her plate and one on Hudson's. "Here, have another. You can microwave it or have it as is."

"I like it as is," Hudson said. "I can taste the flavors more."

His nani was digging through the fridge. "No lime," she announced after a thorough search. "Next time. And we'll make some homemade chutneys to go with them."

"I'd like that." Hudson took a big bite of the samosa. "What about my parents, though?" he asked after he swallowed. He noticed his grandmother watching him.

"You know, beta, you even look a lot like your grandfather," Nani said. "He was a doctor, like your mom, but he loved architecture, like your dad. He introduced your parents when they all worked on a project to design and establish medical clinics in rural areas of India. He was very gifted, very talented. Just like you!"

Hudson smiled meekly.

"Why such a sad smile, beta?" his nani said. "You know you are very talented. You sing, you dance, you're a Broadway STAR! You're a first-generation Indian American Shah Rukh Khan. And you cook and bake and have your own show on FoodTube!"

Hudson grinned as his nani beamed at him. But it lasted only a moment. She was suddenly back on her feet. "What did your mother want you to talk to me about?" she said very seriously.

"What do you mean?" Hudson pretended not to know what she was talking about.

"I heard her whispers," his nani said. "She always thinks I can't hear a word she says, but she also doesn't know that she has always had the loudest whisper. Even when she was small, I could hear her across the house!"

"Oh, she just wanted to make sure you're comfortable and wanted to know if there's anything you n-need . . . ," Hudson stammered.

"Nonsense!" His nani cut him off with a wave of her hand. "I've been living here for over a year, and I'm more than comfortable. What is she up to?"

Hudson knew he was cornered. In fact, he literally had been backed into the corner of the kitchen where two counters met. He couldn't slip away, so he told his grandmother the details of the cupcake competition.

"I don't know what to do about the 'family flavors' part," Hudson said, feeling defeated all over again.

But his grandmother was already in action. "Hudson, beta, your mother never fully mastered my cooking. She has had other priorities with raising her family and being a most excellent doctor." She was beaming with pride now at how much her daughter had accomplished. "But she got her sweet tooth from me, and you got it from her. And you know flavors, so why not create something new? This is a fun challenge!"

Hudson couldn't help but think of how much his nani was sounding like Monica. And before he knew what was happening, his nani had covered the counter with ingredients. She had grabbed eggs and flour, as well as unsalted butter, vanilla extract, semisweet chocolate, salt, granulated sugar, and cream of tartar. "Let's bake!" she said.

"But what are we making?" Hudson said, getting up from the stool himself and eyeing the ingredients.

"You tell me," his nani said mischievously.

"Looks like . . . chocolate something . . ." Hudson racked his brain for what all these ingredients could make. It didn't take him terribly long. "Soufflé!" he exclaimed. "We're making soufflé."

His nani clapped her hands together and stood up on her tiptoes before tucking a strand of her gray hair, which had fallen from her bun, behind her right ear. "Yes!" she said. "I've always wanted to learn, and when your mother told me you know how to make it, I was more than dazzled," she said. "I tried to follow your recipe on FoodTube months ago, but I failed miserably."

"You watch *Broadway Sizzlers*?" Hudson said, his eyes wide.

"Always," she said. "I think the soufflé was on the episode with that young man from *Hamilton*."

"You mean Leslie Odom Jr.?"

"Yes, that's him!"

Hudson glanced at the clock on the microwave. It was getting to be quite late, and he hadn't started his homework yet. He also had to be at the theater early the next day. The Squad had agreed to meet and work on TikTok videos. Soufflé was not easy to make, but Hudson wasn't ready for bed, especially now that he and his nani were talking and laughing. Her excitement was infectious.

"Okay, Nani," he said. "This recipe requires a lot of patience, but let's go for it."

Hudson stepped to the pantry and took a close look inside. "You know, we could make other desserts while the soufflé is baking and cooling. Even simple ones. But maybe we could add some other flavors?"

Nani stepped next to Hudson to examine the various bottles and jars. She pulled out a silver tin and pried open the lid. "This is the best place to start," she said. "The spice box!"

Hudson moved his face close to the box, inhaling the different flavors.

"That one's turmeric, for color, I know," he said, pointing to a bright orange powder. "And that one is simply salt. That's fenugreek."

"And we have cardamom, garam masala, and cumin!" Nani said.

Hudson looked at his nani conspiratorially. "We can add these to all sorts of cookies. Maybe even to a cake!"

"Yes! Let's try it!" Nani smiled widely and bounced excitedly on her toes, like a young girl with a taste for adventure.

Nine

By the time Hudson arrived at the theater, Monica, Relly, and April had already shot and uploaded five TikTok videos. April was committed to filming more, but Monica and Relly wouldn't have it.

"We're tired," Monica told her friend gently.

"And we don't want to oversaturate the social feeds," Relly added, collapsing into a chair backstage. Years ago it had been used as King Arthur's throne in a production of *Camelot*. The scarlet velvet had been reupholstered many times over the years. The legs were solid, and the cushioning was just right. Relly loved that chair and often sat in it, particularly during intermission.

"Where have you been?" April demanded of Hudson after she agreed to give her friends a break. Relly's point about flooding the feeds was a good one.

"Sorry," Hudson said, putting down his stuffed backpack and pulling from it a box of pistachio macarons and a separate box of red velvet macarons. He then produced a box of coconut macaroons. Hudson had never brought so many treats to the theater at once.

"What's all this?" April asked, amazed at the spread before her.

"More macarons!" Relly exclaimed, coming closer. "That looks like red velvet. My favorite!" He leaped off the comfy chair to take a closer look but then stopped short.

"Every flavor is your favorite, isn't it?" Hudson said.

"Hudson, you look exhausted," Relly said. "Did you even sleep?"

Hudson smiled, though his smile turned into a yawn. "Not really," he admitted. "I was up late . . . working."

"Oh, did you finally get caught up on your homework?" Monica asked. The Squad often consulted each other on homework over text and even video chats at night, but lately Hudson hadn't taken part.

"Sort of," Hudson said. "Well, I got up early to do homework."

April cut him off as she crossed her arms. "So why are

you late for our TikTok meeting if you were up early?"

Hudson knew his friend would not like his answer. "Honestly?" he asked.

"Honestly. Were you late because you were baking all this?" She waved her right arm around the spread of treats Hudson had brought. She couldn't help herself—she licked her lips at the sight of the deliciousness before her.

"No. I fell back asleep," Hudson admitted.

"It's important to get good sleep," Relly said. "My grandfather is always saying, 'You're going to have two left feet if you don't get sleep.'" He tapped his feet and did a twirl.

"Where did all this come from, then?" April was persistent.

Hudson didn't waffle. He knew it wouldn't do any good. "I didn't make them this morning. I made those last night. With my grandmother."

"You made all this last night?" It was Relly's turn to express disbelief.

"We stayed up really late. We also made chocolate soufflé from scratch. And a white layer cake with chocolate buttercream. Ideally it would have been marshmallow, but we didn't have the right ingredients for that. And it was too late to get groceries."

Relly, Monica, and April were now all lined up in front of Hudson, amazed and speechless.

When his friends didn't respond, Hudson continued. "My grandmother was having a hard time understanding the difference between macaroons and macarons. She had wanted to make macarons after she saw the strawberry ones I made recently, but she was pronouncing it 'macaroons.' So we ended up with macaroons before realizing the mistake. Then we made the pistachio and red velvet macarons. She never knew they were two different desserts."

Hudson took a seat on the floor and smiled at the memory. He shook his head as he recalled his grandmother's surprise at learning there were two completely different desserts with such similar names.

All of a sudden, Claudia and Artie blew through the back of the theater where the Squad had been chatting.

"Okay, okay," Artie said. It was chilly backstage, but beads of sweat were falling down his forehead. His salt-and-pepper hair was standing up all over the place, and his scarf was coming undone. "We have a problem," he began, but Claudia cut him off.

"It's not a problem, really, Artie," she said, laughing nervously, her red cat-eye glasses sliding down her nose.

"Well, I just got back from lunch with Rick Gallo. He doesn't know if he should continue to invest in *Our Time*. I consider that a problem." Artie spun around to face Claudia.

"Are we in trouble?" the Squad asked all at once.

"We could be if Slick Rick pulls out of the show," Artie said.

The Squad looked at each other in confusion. "But we're always so busy," Monica said. "We've got a packed house every night!"

Artie shook his head vigorously, sending sweat flying. Hudson quickly covered the box of red velvet macarons, which Relly had already opened.

"We're busy, but things can change on Broadway in an instant," Artie said. "Being the best now doesn't mean you're always the best!" He paused and looked at the Squad carefully. "Especially not with *Move It!* coming up."

"What this means," Claudia said before the kids could really absorb what Artie had told them, "is that we really have to step. It. Up." She snapped her fingers to emphasize the last three words.

"We need more TikTok videos!" April exclaimed, pulling out her phone, ready to record at a moment's notice.

"No, we need more rehearsing," Claudia said. "To the stage!" She pointed toward the main stage, like a general leading the charge in battle. Maria was there waiting for them. "I'd like to chat with Hudson," Claudia said, ushering the other children along with Artie. "Just for a moment."

April, Relly, and Monica glanced at each other quickly and then smiled at Hudson. Monica reached over and squeezed his hand quickly. Then Hudson was alone with Claudia.

"Hudson, dear," she said. "Your timing has been better, but it's still just a bit off, especially in the waterfall scene. Remember, it's important to stay on beat, or you'll throw your castmates off. And if one person gets lost, well, the entire group gets lost. Okay?"

Hudson didn't have to be told twice. He knew he was the least polished of the group, and his costume felt tighter these days. All the sugar he and his grandmother had tasted last night wasn't helping. And today he was so tired.

"I got it, Claudia," he said, mustering as much cheerfulness as possible. "I don't want to let everyone down."

Claudia nodded once. "You also don't want to let yourself down." She turned quickly to join the others onstage.

Hudson gathered up the treats and quickly placed them in a neat pile. He caught his reflection in a mirror. "Wow," he said to himself, "I do look beat. I'll need extra makeup to cover those circles under my eyes."

"Hudson, they're waiting for you." Hudson saw Jimmy's reflection in the mirror.

"On my way, Jimmy." Hudson turned to head to the stage but then stopped. "Hey, Jimmy, remember when you told me 'There's no place like home'?"

"Sure I do."

"Well, thanks. It turns out you're right."

Jimmy nodded. "It's true, Hudson. This theater—Broadway, really—is my home. Ethel Merman took a chance on me, and I would be lost without all of it." He looked toward the stage, where Maria was tapping her foot impatiently. "You better hustle."

The Squad rehearsed all afternoon, and, once again excited about their progress, they uploaded a TikTok video.

This one featured Monica. "We're ready for another great show!" she sang to show off her voice. "It's certainly *Our Time!*"

They weren't able to eat properly before the show started. But the whole cast was running on adrenaline, and Hudson didn't feel much like eating.

"I'll have something at intermission," he promised Monica. She squeezed his hand again just before the curtain went up. That initial flash of lights illuminating them never got old.

The first act went smoothly, and Hudson did have a couple of bites of a sandwich at intermission. But, almost immediately, he wished he hadn't. The sugar from earlier wasn't sitting well during the second act.

The problems began when Hudson lost his balance while doing a barrel turn—the same move he and his friends had been rehearsing before the show. He somehow tripped over himself, getting his right leg caught behind his left leg. He landed in the waterfall, eliciting laughter from the audience and splashing Monica, Relly, and April, who had no choice but to keep going.

"The show must go on," Hudson muttered to himself.

Somehow, the Squad made it through the rest of the show, with Hudson soaking wet and the entire Squad trying not to slip in the trail of water he left all over the stage.

As soon as the curtain went down, Claudia ran to the kids. Artie was nowhere to be found—he had hidden in his office as soon as Hudson tripped and wasn't even aware yet that the waterfall had become the star of act two.

"H-H-Hudson," Claudia stammered, somewhat hysterical. Her usually perfect updo was now disheveled, and her bright red lipstick was completely smudged from biting her knuckles, which were also covered in red. Her eyeliner was also a mess.

Before she could say anything else, Hudson cut her off. "I'm doing my best!" he yelled. He ran to his dressing room and grabbed his backpack and windbreaker, not even bothering to change out of his soaking-wet costume.

"Hudson, wait!" It was Monica.

But Hudson wasn't stopping. He was determined to get out of the Ethel Merman as soon as possible. Though the show had hardly ended, several eager fans had already made their way to the stage door, lining up for autographs.

"There's only so much one person can do!"

"You know it's going to be jam-packed if you go that way, kid," Jimmy said, gesturing to the stage door.

Without a word, Hudson ran to the front of the theater, rushing past the grand statue of Ethel Merman. He stopped in front of it. The inscription, a quote from the famed Broadway star, had caught his eye.

Hudson read it aloud. "'Be yourself—it's the one thing you can do better than anyone else.'" He looked up at the statue's face. He could swear she winked.

Hudson was startled. He closed his eyes briefly and looked back at the statue's face. It seemed just like a statue again. By now the lobby had cleared. Hudson ran down the front steps and pushed open the doors, avoiding the audience. He made his way home as quickly as he could.

Ten

The phone rang at the Patel residence early the next morning. They still kept a landline as a backup on the off chance that Dr. Patel's cell phone didn't work when she was on call.

"Hudson!" Sudhir yelled from the kitchen, where the rest of the family was enjoying a breakfast of idlis and chutneys. Hudson's nani had made the South Indian dish, small cakes made from rice and lentil batter, from scratch. "It's for you!"

"Don't yell!" his mother scolded. "You'll wake the neighbors."

"You'll wake the whole Upper West Side," his father said as he helped himself to another idli.

"Poor Hudson must be so tired," his nani said. "I kept him up late the other night. He taught me how to bake!"

"Go wake your brother. Tell him to pick up the phone in the master bedroom." Hudson's mother shooed her younger son off his chair and toward the bedroom the two boys shared. "And stop rolling your eyes. I can see you, you know."

Hudson's brother slumped to the back of the apartment and swung open the bedroom door.

Hudson was lying on his stomach, his limbs askew. He was snoring softly.

"Hudson!" his brother shouted. "Wake up!"

Hudson didn't answer. He only groaned and then rolled onto his side.

"Hudson!" his brother yelled again. "You have a phone call." Now Sudhir stepped forward and quickly swiped his finger along the bottom of his brother's exposed foot.

"Stop!" Hudson yelled, bolting upright. "That tickles." He collapsed back on the bed and pulled a plush blue throw blanket off the floor and over his head.

"That's the point," Sudhir said. "You have to get up. You have a phone call."

Hudson peeked out from under the blanket. He thought for a moment and then pulled his head back under the blanket. "Tell them I'm not here," he said, his voice muffled. He knew it had to be someone calling about the show—either someone from the Squad or Claudia or even Artie. All of them had tried to reach him on his cell phone the night before, but he had refused to answer them. He had finally shut off his phone and thrown it under his bed.

Sudhir again ran his finger over the underside of Hudson's foot, which was still exposed, but Hudson simply jerked his foot away. Other than that, he wouldn't budge. Sudhir skipped back to the kitchen, adjusting his glasses as he went.

"Hudson won't come to the phone." His tone was gloating, as he knew his mother would not like Hudson's apparent rudeness.

Their mother walked to the phone and picked it up. "Hello?" she said into the receiver. "Oh, Claudia! It's nice to hear from you. It's been so long since we've talked."

Everyone at the table stopped to listen. It was rare for Claudia to call these days, and they knew it wasn't good news when Hudson's mom started chewing on her lower lip.

"Oh dear," she muttered at one point, prompting

Hudson's father and his nani to exchange concerned glances across the table.

"Thank you for calling, Claudia," Dr. Patel said. "I'll make sure Hudson gets some rest. And that he calls his friends. I am sure they are very concerned."

The family watched Hudson's mother hang up the phone and then settle back into her chair at the table. Sudhir was the first to speak.

"Aren't you going to yell at him?" he said, eager for some drama. He knew rudeness was not tolerated in their household, and he considered it rude that Hudson had not come to the phone for Claudia.

"He's had a rough few days," Hudson's mother said, dipping her idli into a green coconut chutney.

"Oooohhh, what happened?" his brother asked.

"Mind your own business, Sudhir," his mother snapped. "And leave your brother alone today. Let him rest."

Hudson's father looked at his wife across the table with his eyebrows furrowed. "Shouldn't Hudson be going to the theater today?"

Hudson's mother picked up her plate and tilted her head toward the living room. "Let's chat in there," she said. "You stay here," she snapped at Sudhir. "No spying. Help your grandmother with your sister."

Nisha was in her high chair, alternately smashing her

idli with her fists and then balling it with her hands. Her face was smeared with imli and coconut chutney. She was cooing between bites of food.

Hudson's father followed his mother into the living room. He turned on the TV and adjusted the volume so it was just loud enough to muffle their voices; he knew Sudhir would try to listen in on their conversation, despite the explicit directive not to.

"Hudson won't be starring in the show tonight." Hudson's mother explained the waterfall mishap from the night before. "He was very tired yesterday, and Claudia said she and Artie agree that he needs to get some rest. They think he may need to take at least two, even three days off." She lowered her voice and leaned close to her husband. "Especially with *Move It!* getting so much attention."

"So, who will be playing my part tonight?" Hudson asked from the doorway.

"Jacob will be taking on your part tonight."

Hudson barely made it the few steps to the closest chair, a huge recliner the color of an apricot, before collapsing. The chair practically swallowed him up. If he sat in it properly, his feet would just barely touch the ground, but now he slumped down in it so low that his legs extended far in front of him.

His dad guessed what he was thinking. "Hudson, beta,

Jacob will do a great job." He pushed aside his collection of large architecture-themed coffee table books and leaned on the edge of a sturdy side table next to Hudson. "He is very committed to the show. He will play your character well. Everyone knows that he has worked very hard learning your part—and Relly's." He put his hand on his son's shoulder, but Hudson shrugged it away.

"Relly has never had Jacob perform for him," he burst out. "I don't want to be the first one of the Squad to have an understudy take my place."

Hudson's father reached out for his son again. "Someone has to be first. It's bound to happen at some point," he said. Hudson shrugged him off again, so he sat on the couch and leaned toward his son. "Someone could get sick or hurt. In this case, you are very tired and need to rest."

Hudson's mother set her empty plate aside and sat next to her husband on the couch. "You know, Hudson," she said, "there's nothing wrong with taking a break."

Hudson glared at his parents, gritting his teeth. The thought of Jacob taking his place was excruciating. He was about to protest again, but Claudia had made the decision already, so there was no point.

"It's Saturday, and it's Diwali, Hudson," his mother said. "Now that you don't have to rush to the theater, let's all take a little time out before we go to the festival tonight."

Hudson was silent. He glanced over at the television, which was showing a nature documentary about hummingbirds. His nani poked her head into the room from the kitchen, and Hudson's frustration immediately melted away.

"Will you be joining us today?" he asked Nani.

She gracefully stepped into the room and struck a classic bharata natyam pose, one she had mastered in her dancing studies when she was about Hudson's age. "Of course I will!" she said. "It's Diwali, after all, and we have so much to do!"

"I guess that's that, then," Hudson said excitedly. "Let me get dressed." He got up and started heading toward the bathroom to wash up.

"Yes, get dressed and have some breakfast," his nani said. "We have fresh idli. But hurry before your father and brother eat them all!"

They all laughed.

"But first, Hudson," his mother said, stopping her son, "call your friends. They're worried about you."

Eleven

Hudson needed a few minutes to clear his head. So much had happened in the past few days, and he was indeed very tired. And he didn't know what he was going to say to his friends.

He showered and dressed carefully in jeans and a red checkered shirt over a white T-shirt and selected his favorite gray sneakers. He combed his hair, and then he finally picked up his phone. He hesitated before turning it on, then set it down on the nightstand.

"I'll make the bed first," he said to himself.

It took him longer than it should have to tuck in the sheets and fluff the pillows, but only because he was trying to replicate the nearly perfect job that Sudhir had done on his own bed.

Done is better than perfect, he finally told himself.

He grabbed his phone and sat down on top of the bed, rumpling the covers. He took a deep breath, cradling the phone in his hands.

"Okay, let's get to it," he said out loud, turning on the phone, feeling ready now to face what he knew would be a deluge of messages and missed calls from April, Relly, and Monica. He was right. There were sixty-seven text messages, both to Hudson alone and to the entire group chat, as well as seventeen missed calls and five voicemails—one from each friend, plus one from Claudia and another from Artie. Those voicemails were a big deal. No one ever left voicemails.

Hudson scanned through the group messages quickly and was about to listen to the voicemails when a call came through. It was Monica.

"Hudson! Finally! We are really worried about you. Are you okay?"

"I'm okay," Hudson said, suddenly feeling sad and disappointed again. "Tired, but good."

"Where is he?" Hudson could hear Relly yelling in the background. He could tell his friend was also very concerned.

"He's at home," Monica replied.

"Tell him we're coming over." This time it was April's voice he heard.

"How about I meet you out?" Hudson said before Monica even asked if they could come to his house. "There's just a lot going on here today."

"We're at the Ethel Merman right now," Monica said. "Do you want to meet us here?"

Hudson was silent. The thought of going to the theater was upsetting, especially if there was a chance he might run into Jacob, Claudia, or Artie.

"Hudson, are you still there?" Monica said, the worry in her voice palpable. "I can't hear you."

"Yeah, I'm here," he said.

"Claudia told us about tonight's performance," Monica continued. "It's okay. We're not upset."

"Even April isn't upset?" Hudson asked.

"No," Monica said emphatically. "We get it. You're overwhelmed."

"Well, now it's time for Jacob's big break," Hudson said. "I'm worried he'll end up replacing me."

Monica laughed. "Don't worry about that, Hudson. You're unique. Just tell us where to meet you."

Suddenly, Hudson realized that his stomach was rumbling. "Let me eat breakfast really quick, and I'll text you."

He went to the living room, which was empty, but the

television was turned on to the local news.

"The hottest new musical to hit Broadway in quite some time is still in rehearsals, but the cast has been making surprise appearances all over the city," a reporter said. "And today is no different. Led by Tabitha Fox, they're entertaining tourists and locals alike with a subway performance. . . ."

Hudson switched off the TV. He went to the kitchen, where Sudhir was intently doing his science homework, his father was reading the *Wall Street Journal*, and his nani was writing out a list.

"Where's Mom?" Hudson asked as he took his seat at the table and helped himself to two idlis and some sambar.

"She's cleaning up your sister," his nani said, smiling. "Those little ones always make such a mess at that age."

Hudson swallowed a big piece of idli and turned to his father. "I'm going to meet the Squad for a bit," he said. "Claudia told them—"

"Oooohhhh, they're going to be so mad at you!" Hudson's brother interrupted. "You're the first to need an understudy."

Their father, normally a joyful, quiet man, gave his younger son a piercing look that made it clear he had crossed a line. Hudson's brother shrank back and picked up his books.

"Sorry, Hudson," he said, without having to be told. Then he got up and scampered back to their bedroom to finish his homework.

"Hudson, beta, don't listen to him," his father began, carefully folding the newspaper and placing it back on the table.

"It's okay, Dad," Hudson said. "I already talked to Monica, and she said that none of them are upset. She told me that she understands and that everyone needs some rest sometimes."

"Even April agrees?" his father said, cocking an eyebrow and furrowing his brow before grinning a little.

Hudson laughed. "Yeah, even April agrees. You know, Dad, I've seen her catnapping at the theater, and she sometimes says things about how she needs to catch up on her sleep."

"We all need that, but especially at your age," Hudson's nani chimed in. "Especially kids like you! So busy all the time, running from activity to activity and performing all the time. It's exciting, but I can't imagine how you do it all."

Hudson devoured a third idli, plain this time, as the sambar—his father's favorite part of the meal—was gone. Hudson was taking his plate to the sink when his mother walked into the kitchen with Nisha, now sleeping, cradled over her shoulder.

"I don't think we'll have time for a big dinner before the Diwali festival," she said. "There will be plenty of food there, so maybe we should just have some snacks instead and save the big dinner for later in the week?"

"That works for me," Nani said. "We're out of most of our spices, anyway."

"How? We had so much!" Hudson's mom was bewildered.

Hudson exchanged glances with his nani. During their late-night baking session, they had used up most of the spices by adding them to the desserts. A hint of turmeric for color here and there, a dash of fenugreek seeds for an earthy flavor, and cumin seeds for a nutty one.

"I can get them," Hudson interjected before his nani could try to explain. He hadn't asked his mother's permission to use her spices, and he thought it only fair that he replace what he had used.

"Excellent!" Nani said. "I made a list of what we need while you were eating. But where will you go? There's not enough time to go to the shops I like in Queens."

"You don't have to go to Queens," Hudson's mother said. "Go to Kalustyan's. They have everything, and you won't have to leave Manhattan."

Hudson's father laughed. "Ah, Kalustyan's," he said, interlacing his fingers behind his head and tipping his chair back slightly as a big smile crossed his face. "How

IN THE MIX

much time did we spend there while you were doing your fellowship at NYU?" he said, turning to his wife.

"A lot of time," she responded, smiling back at her husband. "That deli upstairs was a great place for a break and something to eat."

"Well, it sounds like Kalustyan's will be the perfect place to get the spices in a pinch," Nani said.

She turned to her grandson and handed him the shopping list. Hudson noted how organized it was. *I'll have to make my list this good for the cupcake competition,* he thought.

But Nani was leaning over his shoulder, pointing at the end of the list. "If you can't find this last one, don't worry— for now."

Hudson looked quizzically at what his nani had written. "What is it?" he asked.

"Just ask if they have it at the store. It's a surprise." He caught a twinkle in her eye.

"Hudson, be back in time to get ready for the festival, okay?" his mother called after him as she rose from the table.

"Okay!" he said as the apartment door closed behind him.

Twelve

Let's meet in Kips Bay, Hudson texted Monica as he walked toward the subway.

Where's that? she texted back.

East Side, in the 20s.

Can you be more specific? Even after living in the city for a year, Monica was still learning the names of the different neighborhoods.

Well, it's near Curry Hill, Hudson began, but then he realized that description would likely not mean much to Monica—or to April or even Relly. Let's meet at 24th and Lexington—right outside Baruch College. It was the best landmark Hudson could think of. Or maybe just meet me in Madison Square Park. The subway will drop you right there at 23rd Street. Take your time, though—it's going to take me a bit to get there on the train.

Raised in the city, Hudson knew all the subway stops offhand for the main train lines, particularly those that ran through Manhattan. His knowledge of the outer boroughs was not quite as sharp. But he knew that Relly, a true New York native, born and raised in Harlem, would make sure the Squad made it to the right place safely.

The 1 train to Times Square came pretty quickly, and Hudson even got a seat. As he settled in, he suddenly remembered the news clip he'd seen earlier about the *Move It!* cast performing in the subway.

I should have told Monica not to go to the Times Square stop—that's got to be where they were! Hudson slapped his palm on his forehead. But when he got to that station to change to the N/R line to Twenty-Third Street, he didn't see any performers besides a woman dressed as a ballerina and painted silver from head to toe. She would only move if given change. "The *Move It!* performance must have been in Grand Central," Hudson muttered to himself with relief, thinking of the other most likely packed subway spot that would get a lot of attention.

He was lucky again with the timing of the train and made it to Madison Square Park not too long after April, Monica, and Relly. He paused for a moment to take in the

Flatiron, a building his architect father had taught him to admire, and then found his friends in the small park. Monica and Relly were seated on a bench, while April was testing out a new dance move in front of them. She was the first to see Hudson, and she greeted him with a big hug.

"Hey, Hudson," she said. "We were worried about you."

"We *are* worried about you," Relly corrected. "Jacob is over the moon with excitement about performing, but it won't be the same show without you."

"But we're more worried because we know you're feeling overwhelmed," Monica interjected.

Hudson was grateful that his friends were being so supportive. "You know," he began, "the inscription on the Ethel Merman statue caught my eye. 'Be yourself—it's the one thing you can do better than anyone else.'"

"And . . . ," Relly said, waiting for more.

But Hudson wasn't really sure what to say. Monica tried to help.

"You really care about the cupcake competition, don't you?" she said.

"Yes." Hudson felt like he could speak freely now. "Once that competition is over, I will have so much time again. But I really want to win."

April, Relly, and Monica were quiet for a moment. Finally, Monica spoke. "Winning that competition could change everything for you, especially since you love baking so much."

"Yeah," April added. "If you win, will you still have space for *Our Time*?"

No one said anything for several moments. Instead, the Squad watched a large brown squirrel approach them.

Relly turned to Hudson. "How's the cupcake recipe coming along, anyway?"

"Well . . . ," Hudson began. "It hasn't really."

"What do you mean?" April said fiercely. "You want to win, but you haven't started yet?"

"No." Hudson hesitated. "I've started. My grandmother is helping me learn more about the flavors used in Indian food. She's showing me how she's used them in really creative ways in her recipes. It's cool, but I still don't have my own unique recipe yet."

"Can we help?" Monica asked.

Hudson started leading his friends east.

"Actually, that's partly why I wanted to meet down here," Hudson said. "I didn't want to go to the theater, but I also have some shopping to do."

Relly stopped short. "I hate shopping!" He groaned. "I'm the kind of person that wants to get in and out. I know what I need and that's it."

"We're not shopping for clothes, Relly," Hudson said,

lightly punching his friend in the shoulder. "We're looking for spices."

Now Hudson had Relly's attention. "Food shopping is something else entirely," he said, rubbing his hands together. "I could shop for food all day."

"We're focused on spices today, though. This place also has a café upstairs," Hudson said.

"Well, perfect then. We can shop and eat all at once!" April said.

The Squad continued walking east, avoiding Twenty-Third Street, busy with passing cars and buses and sidewalks jam-packed with pedestrians. Instead, they took Twenty-Fourth Street. On this crisp fall day, it was a wind tunnel. Monica's curls flew around so wildly that she had to do her best to hold her hair back with her hands. Even April's hair, tied in a tight bun, threatened to come loose.

Once the four friends hit Lexington Avenue, they headed north, passing several Indian restaurants that Hudson and his family had visited many times before. It was these restaurants that gave the area the name "Curry Hill." Finally, they arrived at Kalustyan's.

The Squad walked into the store. They all gasped. From floor to ceiling, the shelves contained everything Hudson could need. There were lentils, spices, bags of rice, yogurts, dried fruits, nuts, honey, and other sweeteners—most products were from the Middle East and South Asia. There was even a section for cookware.

"Who knew there was so much inside!" Monica exclaimed.

There were several shoppers in the store, and the woman at the register was busy ringing people up. Hudson pulled out the list Nani had given him and found someone to help him. "Most of these are spices," the worker explained, taking a close look at the list.

He headed toward that section of the store and helped the Squad find the cumin, fenugreek, cardamom, and coriander. He also helped them pick out dal and the right kind of basmati rice. Hudson also got a few extra items, including some vanilla extract, which he always needed for his baking projects, as well as some chutney and achar that looked interesting.

"What's this?" Monica asked him, holding up a small cone she had found near the register.

"That's henna!" April said excitedly. "It makes temporary tattoos."

"It's more than that," Hudson elaborated. "It's a paste made from crushed leaves. You can make really intricate designs, but you have to leave the henna on for hours to let it set. When you rinse off the paste, the design left behind can last for days—weeks even." He picked up a tube. "I actually should get some of that for my mom," he said. "We use it for big celebrations, like weddings and Diwali. We're celebrating it today."

"It's Diwali?" Monica asked. "Isn't that the Festival of Lights you told us about?"

"Yes, it is!" Hudson was happy she had remembered. But suddenly he got worried. "Oh no!" he exclaimed. "What time is it?"

"It's nearly one p.m.," Relly said. "Why? What's wrong?"

"I've got to get home! There's a Diwali festival today. My mom is going to be really upset if I'm late."

"I guess we don't have time to eat, after all." Relly was disappointed.

"We can help you get these things home," Monica offered. "It's a lot to carry on your own, even if you take a taxi."

Hudson nodded. "Okay," he said. He quickly scanned the list his nani had given him to make sure he had gotten everything. "Wait," he said. "I'm missing something."

"What is it?" April was ready to find someone to help again.

"I'm not sure. My grandmother just said to ask the staff here for it, but she didn't seem too convinced they would have it."

The young guy who had helped them earlier was

nowhere to be found. Hudson approached the woman at the register. She had kind, gray eyes lined with thick black kohl. She pursed her lips and raised one eyebrow when she looked at what Hudson's grandmother had written.

She shook her head. "I don't have that," she said. "That's a very special item."

"But this is a specialty store," Hudson said, amused and frustrated all at once. "Do you have anything like it that I can take instead?"

"Anything I have will certainly disappoint. If someone is asking for this exact thing, they are a very good cook."

Now she really had Hudson's attention. "What is it?"

The woman leaned in very close, as if sharing a secret. Her pink dupatta spilled onto the counter as she nearly whispered, "It's a chili pepper." She handed the paper back to Hudson. "Very special."

"Have you ever had it?" Hudson asked.

"Oh no, not me," the woman said. "But I have heard the stories. It does not disappoint."

Hudson was confused. "If I want to get it, where can I find it?"

"That I do not know," the kind woman said. "I have never seen it in New York. I've actually never seen it in person before."

She rang up the groceries, and the Squad left the store.

"We should really take a taxi," Hudson said, worried about the time. He nearly dropped the large bag of rice he had hauled to the end of the block as he hailed a cab heading west. Once they had all piled into the car, Hudson gave the driver his home address.

"We're in a bit of a rush, so please take the fastest route possible," Hudson said politely. He again sat in the front seat, the bag of rice on his lap.

The driver, a Sikh with a grand raspberry-red turban and a magnificent gray beard, turned to cut through to the West Side. It was the same route Hudson had taken alone on the bus several days earlier, but in the daylight, it was refreshing rather than depressing.

"There's Strawberry Fields!" Hudson pointed out the window. "I once thought it was literally a strawberry patch, where you could pick fresh strawberries. Then I learned about John Lennon and the Beatles."

Before they knew it, the taxi had arrived at Hudson's home. "Happy Diwali, Hudson," the driver said as Hudson pulled out his wallet to pay the fare. "No charge. Today is a day to celebrate, and this ride is my gift to you and your friends."

Hudson's jaw hung slack as he stared wide-eyed at the man. "Th-thank you," he stammered. "But how do you know my name?"

The man laughed, pulling at the end of his mustache with his left hand, his elbow resting on the door. "I'm a big fan of *Broadway Sizzlers*. Sometimes I try to make the desserts like you do, but I don't have enough time before my wife comes home and shoos me out of the kitchen." He laughed again. "But she'll at least watch your show with me.'"

Hudson smiled, but he didn't know what to say. "I'm really glad you like my show, sir," he managed.

"Oh no, no, no. No 'sir,'" the man said. "I'm Gian Singh Giani. You can call me G.G."

Hudson nodded and stuck out his hand. "I'm happy to meet you, G.G.," he said. "I hope you and your family have a very happy Diwali. Maybe we'll meet again. . . ." Hudson was about to suggest that G.G. and his wife could be guests on his show but stopped himself. This man was still a stranger, after all.

"Here is my card for my family's business," G.G. said. "We have groceries in Queens."

Hudson was about to ask more about the store. But Relly interrupted. "Hey, Hudson," he nudged. "It's getting late. Won't your mom be waiting?"

"Thank you again," Hudson said to G.G. "Happy Diwali!"

He picked up the sack of rice and walked to the steps, where his friends were waiting with the other groceries.

"What was all that about?" Monica asked.

Hudson explained about the complimentary ride and how G.G. was a fan of his show.

"Ooohhh, don't you love getting recognized?" April said excitedly. "Did you give him your autograph?"

"No," Hudson said, unlocking the door to the building and holding it open for his friends. "I didn't even think about it. And he didn't ask."

The Squad waited for the elevator—it was slow, but the bags would be cumbersome on the stairs. When they entered the Patel residence, they were met with a big commotion. Nisha was crying, and Hudson's father, dressed in a fine blueberry-blue suit and grapefruit-pink tie, was trying to soothe her. Sudhir, in a saffron kurta with gold embroidery, was drinking a glass of orange juice. The sounds of an abandoned video game blared from the living room. Hudson's mother, trailed closely by his nani, walked into the kitchen just as the Squad walked in through the front door. They all stopped short upon spotting one another.

Hudson and his friends took in the sight of his mother. She was dressed in a banana-yellow silk sari with heavy gold embroidery and details of small red and blue flowers. Her long hair was pulled back in a fishtail braid. She wore gold chandelier earrings and a matching gold necklace. On her right wrist was a thick gold bracelet adorned with a vibrant blue peacock.

"There you are!" she said, letting out a big sigh. "I was getting worried." She furrowed her brow at Hudson and looked fiercely at the clock, then back at her son.

"You are so . . . *regal*," April said, unable to take her eyes off Hudson's mother. "Your outfit is stunning!"

"You really are beautiful," Monica added, entranced. "I've never seen anything like it!"

"Thank you, girls," Hudson's mother said, flattered. Her mood softened. "It's so good to see you both. And you, too, Relly." She gestured for the kids to come into the apartment. "Close the door. Put down all those bags. Make yourselves comfortable."

"Yes, yes, come in, come in!" Nani stepped farther into the kitchen. She had on a plum sari, also embroidered in gold but not quite as intricate as her daughter's. She also wore gold bangles and earrings. Her gray hair was pulled back in a tight bun, as usual. "I'm so happy to see you all," she said, taking the baby, now quiet, from her son-in-law. "Harshdev and his friends—always a glorious sight."

"Harshdev?" Relly said. "Who's that?"

"That's me." April, Monica, and Relly turned to Hudson. "That's my real name."

"Really?" Monica asked, intrigued. "It's lovely. Does it mean something?"

"It means 'happiness' or 'delight.'" His nani jumped in,

ever eager to explain and understand the origin of names. "Because our Harshdev brings us so much joy."

"Why do you go by 'Hudson,' then?" Monica asked.

"Well, when I was younger, no one could say my name properly at school, including the teachers," Hudson began.

"He was obsessed with the Hudson River and wanted me to take him down to see it every day—until the weather got too cold," his father chimed in. "One day, he insisted on being called 'Hudson,' so the name stuck."

"I like Harshdev, too," Monica said.

"Yeah, that's really cool," Relly said. "It's different. Unique. I like it."

"Well, everyone knows me as 'Hudson' now," Hudson said.

Nisha cooed in her nani's arms.

April stepped closer to take a look at her. "Even she has beautiful bangles on! They're so colorful!"

Hudson's mother smiled at April. "We still need to get her dressed. We're going to put her in this pink lehenga." She picked up the miniature outfit, a long skirt and matching top, also embroidered in gold thread, and showed it to the Squad. "It matches my husband's tie perfectly," she said. "He's in charge of her today, and with the matching colors, he can't lose her."

"Oh my gosh, how cute!" April said, reaching out to run her fingers over the gold thread and smooth silk.

"Your outfit is pretty cool too," Relly said, examining Sudhir's kurta closely. "That's really nice detail." He whistled.

"You know," Hudson's mother said, suddenly turning her full attention to the Squad. "Why don't you kids all come with us to the festival? I think you'll really enjoy it."

"Oh, that would be so great!" April bounced up and down on her toes.

"But we've got a show tonight, remember?" Relly said.

The Squad was suddenly quiet. They were all thinking the same thing: Hudson wasn't performing.

"You could come for just a short time at least, and maybe come back after the show if we're still there," Nani suggested. "If we go early, we'll get the best food, too. And I know how much you all love food." She winked and then carried Nisha out of the room to dress her.

"Are you sure it's okay if we come?" Monica asked, turning to Hudson's mother. "Especially dressed in leggings and T-shirts?"

"You are welcome just as you are," Hudson's mother said. She took a good look at the two girls. "Unfortunately, I don't have any outfits that will fit you. But I do have some colorful plastic bangles that should. And some bindis. You'll like wearing those!"

"What's a bindi?" Monica asked.

Hudson's mother pointed to the spot between her eyebrows. "It's a decoration that sits right here," she said. "If it's a plain red circle, it's likely an indication of marriage. But we also wear them as fancy decorations for celebrations, like today."

Next she turned to Relly, who was standing between her sons. "Relly, you can probably fit into one of Hudson's kurtas. It might be a little big on you, but see what you can find." Then she paused. "In fact, you girls might also fit into Hudson's clothes. It will just look like a long shirt over your leggings."

She turned to Hudson. "Help your friends pick out some clothes. I'll get the jewelry for the girls. Go quickly! We're running late!"

Less than an hour later, the Patel family and the Squad walked into a large event center in Chelsea. Everyone was now dressed in some form of Indian clothing—Hudson had changed into a kurta that matched his brother's, while Relly was wearing a maroon one. Monica wore a green one, and April had on a purple one. As the youngest and smallest of the Squad, she ended up borrowing it from Sudhir, as Hudson's swallowed her up.

Everyone was excited. Even the baby, ever fidgety, was quiet, taking in the sight of flower mandalas made of sand

and diyas lit everywhere—on tables, on ledges, on the floor, on special lampstands. They were early, and a bharata natyam performance, originating from South India, was in progress. It soon gave way, however, to a Gujarati garba dance. Monica and April joined the fun, while Hudson and Relly went straight for the food. There were samosas and a variety of chutneys, as well as tandoori chicken, paneer tikka, bhajia, and more. And those were just the appetizers.

"Hudson, pay attention to the mithai." It was Nani. She nudged her grandson toward the dessert table, which was overflowing with gulab jamun, laddoos, rasgullas, chum chums, halwa, jalebis, kheer—it was endless. "But," she added, looking at him fiercely, "be sure to consider *all* the flavors you taste." With that, she headed toward the dance floor.

Hmmmm . . . , Hudson thought. He looked at what was on his plate already: two samosas with imli. *What can I do with this imli?*

"What's imli?" Relly asked, reading a label on the table. April and Monica, now getting food themselves after the garba dance gave way to a Punjabi bhangra performance, came closer to take a look.

"It's tamarind sauce," Hudson explained, pointing at the dark brown sauce on his plate. "I usually only eat it with samosas, but now I wonder . . ." His voice trailed off as he walked toward the dessert table. He stood there for a long time, examining what was on the table. Finally, he picked up his favorites, gulab jamun and laddoos. He broke off a piece of each with a fork and dipped them in the tamarind sauce. *Tangy*, he thought after taking a bite. *The laddoo has promise since it's not so messy.* The gulab jamun—a fried ball of dough soaked in syrup—was better on its own, while the laddoo, also a round sweet but without syrup, was more malleable. Hudson could see himself adding other ingredients to it to make it his own.

"What should I try?" Relly asked, looking over the dessert table.

Hudson explained what each dessert was, surprising himself with how much he knew. Between them, his friends took a sample of everything.

"What's this shiny stuff on top?" Monica asked, picking up a piece of kaju ki barfi, which was made of cashew nuts and milk. It was topped with a silver leaf.

"You can eat that," Hudson said. "It's an edible decoration."

"Are you enjoying yourselves?" Hudson's father was selecting his own desserts now. "Mmmmm . . . my favorite. Jalebis. These are best, though, when they are hot and fresh, in a bowl of milk."

"Those are my least favorite," Hudson said. "Too sweet. And there's something about the bright orange color that gets me."

The Squad spent the next two hours immersed in the Diwali festival, watching dances, eating food, and admiring the bright, intricate clothes.

"Hey, it's almost time to get to the theater," Relly said, turning to Monica and April. "We should get going."

"Oh, but this is so much fun." April sighed. She had been posting to her social channels throughout the festival, especially the dances and the clothes. *#DiwaliCelebration*

"We've got to do our jobs, you know," Relly said. "We can't forget about *Move It!*"

"Don't remind her of that right now," Monica warned. "She's in such a good mood."

"It's fine," April said. "Hudson is going to get some rest and be all better. And look, I just got all sorts of new followers with the pictures and videos I've posted in the last few hours. Everyone loves the colors and clothing!"

Monica, Relly, and April said their goodbyes to Hudson and made sure to find every member of his family on their way out.

"Do you want to watch the show tonight?" Hudson's nani asked. "Maybe just to support your friends?"

"No," Hudson said immediately. "I have some ideas I

want your help with. And I don't think I could bear watching Jacob take my place."

"He'll do a great job, Hudson," his nani said. "He takes a lot of pride in his work, and I think he looks up to you and Relly a lot." She turned to watch the dancing again.

"Do you want to join in?" Hudson asked. He had seen her participating in the dandiya raas earlier, but she had been observing most of the afternoon, taking over baby-watching duties from her son-in-law.

"No, beta. It's okay. I've had my fill for today. My knees can't take much more of it these days, but I do love to watch." She looked longingly at the scene before her for a moment before turning to face Hudson directly, a piercing look once again coming over her face.

"You said you have ideas." She took her grandson's hand. "I think it's time to go home." She spotted her daughter and son-in-law on the dance floor. "You know, why don't we get your brother and sister and take them with us? We can let your parents have a good time tonight. They have so little time alone together to have fun."

Hudson watched his parents. "Okay," he agreed. "That sounds like a good plan. But let's keep Sudhir out of the kitchen."

"You have a deal!" his nani said, holding her hand up for a high five.

She walked over to Hudson's parents to tell them the plan while Hudson gathered his siblings. A DJ started to play, mixing techno beats with traditional Indian music. It was scintillating. Hudson took a look around at the attendees; there were all types of people here, from all different backgrounds—not just Indian—celebrating together.

His nani caught the wonder on his face. "Remember, beta, you don't have to live in two worlds."

Thirteen

Back at the apartment, Hudson and his grandmother didn't bother to change out of their fancy festival clothes before starting to mix flavors in the kitchen.

"I really think the imli will go well with something sweet. A little bit of tangy with sweet, you know?" Hudson was saying.

"Good," his grandmother said, perched on a stool at the counter, watching her grandson closely. "What else?"

"Something with laddoos, maybe. I was thinking about gulab jamun, but the syrup will be too messy. And the syrup is key for that dessert to work."

"Okay," his nani said. She thought for a moment, considering the laddoo option. "Was there anything else that caught your eye tonight?"

Now it was Hudson's turn to pause and think. "Well, Monica was really interested in the silver leaf on the barfi. Would silver leaf work on laddoo?"

"Presentation matters, as your architect father will be the first to tell you, I'm sure," his nani said, "but let's focus on the flavors first."

Hudson grabbed a pad of paper and pen that were magnetically attached to the fridge door. He started to make a list.

"Flavors," he said aloud as he wrote. "Sweet—obviously—but also tangy and nutty." He looked up at his nani intently. "And spicy."

She smiled. "If it suits you to have something spicy, then have something spicy," she said mischievously.

"You've been dropping hints about spice, haven't you?" Hudson asked. Now he narrowed his eyes at her.

She giggled. "Did you find out what that surprise was on my grocery list?"

"It's a chili," Hudson said. "That's all I know. We couldn't find it at Kalustyan's, and they didn't know where I can find it in the city. It sounds like it's difficult to get ahold of it."

"Well, they know it exists. That's a good first step," his nani said. She hopped off the stool and shuffled toward the fridge, somehow managing not to trip over the hem of her sari even though she had exchanged her regular shoes for house slippers. From the side door, she picked up a jar of chilis that only Hudson's father usually touched.

"Are you ready for something spicy?" she asked her grandson. "Very hot?"

Hudson hesitated. When he was ten, he explained to her, he had insisted he was old enough to have chilis like his father. His father had finally relented, despite his mother's warnings that she did not approve and wouldn't dare touch them herself. And Hudson had regretted it—he hadn't touched those jars since.

"I've had that before, I think," Hudson said, not sure if these chilis were the same ones he remembered. "I don't think I'll like it."

His nani picked one chili out of the jar. "It's not about liking it," she said. "It's about understanding how the powerful flavor works with other flavors to create something interesting and unique."

"But it's really hot," Hudson blurted out. "I don't think my mouth can take it."

"Let's see what we can do about that." His nani pulled out a piece of dark chocolate—it was from his mom's personal, private stash, which she thought no one knew about. "This chocolate has ninety percent cacao," she said.

She also brought out a jar of homemade imli. She dipped a spoon into it and dripped a little onto the chocolate. Then she cut off a small piece of the chili to top it off.

"Will you try it?" she asked, holding the plate out to her grandson.

Hudson eyed the creation carefully. He was certainly curious. "I'm not sure. Will you try it with me?"

His nani quickly made another treat for herself. She picked it up, and Hudson picked up the other.

"Cheers!" she said, knocking her piece of chocolate against Hudson's. "To trying something new—and spicy!"

She put the entire piece of chocolate in her mouth. Hudson shut his eyes tight and then did the same. It was spicy—very spicy. But the flavors exploded in his mouth. The spice wasn't as intense as he had remembered, though the chili certainly left his mouth feeling hot.

He opened his eyes to find his nani watching him, a playful smile on her mouth, a twinkle in her eye.

"How was that?" she said.

"It was really good," he said. "It was spicy, but that wasn't like what I remembered."

"That's because your father made the mistake of giving you the chili plain. You can't eat something so spicy plain, especially if you're not used to it."

"But he does it all the time!" Hudson said.

"He's done it all his life. I used to be able to eat all that spice, but over time I have lost my taste for it. And honestly, these chilis are not very hot."

"What are they?"

"They're habaneros. You can get them anywhere. But now let's get started on that cupcake recipe. You and your friends brought everything we will need, I think. But you lead. I am just here to help."

Hudson started to whip up cupcake batter with ingredients he always had on hand. He made chocolate, vanilla, and red velvet. For fun, he also added a pumpkin flavor.

Just as he was pulling the finished cupcake bases out of the oven, his parents stumbled through the door, holding hands and laughing, singing "Kabhi Kabhie Mere Dil Mein," a Bollywood song from their childhoods. They didn't notice that anyone else was in the room at first.

Hudson, uncomfortable with this public display of affection, turned away from them and busied himself with cleaning up the mess of flour on the counter. His nani, however, chuckled. Her daughter and son-in-law turned to her, suddenly serious.

"Oh! We didn't notice you were still up," Hudson's mother said. "We were having so much fun at the Diwali festival that we lost track of time." Suddenly she noticed her son was also in the room. "Hudson! Why aren't you in bed? That's the reason Claudia and Artie wanted you home tonight. You need to get some rest."

"It's my fault," Hudson's grandmother interjected before Hudson could say anything. "We started talking about the cupcake competition, and we got carried away. We didn't notice the late hour either."

"Are those fresh cupcakes?" Hudson's father asked, peering at the baked goods on the counter. "May I have one?"

"You had enough mithai at the festival," his wife scolded playfully.

"Those aren't for eating, Dad," Hudson said. "We are going to try some flavors for the competition."

"Leave it for tomorrow," his mother said. "Let them cool, and check in on your friends to see how the performance went tonight. The show must be over by now."

Hudson nodded and turned to his grandmother. "Thanks for helping me tonight," he said. "I have some ideas we should try in the morning."

"You are very welcome, beta," she said. "I'll change and then put these cupcakes away once they have cooled. You check in with your friends. Maybe they will want to be taste-testers." She winked at her grandson and then made her way to the room she shared with Nisha, who had been sleeping soundly since they got home.

Hudson said good night to his parents and headed to

the bedroom he shared with his brother. Light seeped from under the doorway, but that didn't mean his brother was still awake. As usual, Sudhir had fallen asleep reading a comic book.

Hudson gently took the comic book out of his brother's hands and placed it on the nightstand between their beds. He also removed his brother's glasses. He turned off the main light and switched on a small reading light on the nightstand.

He pulled out his phone and sent a group text to the Squad.

How did it go tonight? he wrote.

Relly texted back first. It went pretty well, but Jacob tripped outside. I think his knee's going to be purple tomorrow.

The fans were asking about you after the show, Monica texted. They wanted to know where you were.

We also heard Artie talking about Slick Rick again, April wrote. It sounds like we really might be in trouble.

Suddenly another text came through—this one was from Claudia.

Hudson, I was about to call, but I thought you might be resting. I hope you have been resting. We need you back tomorrow. There's all this buzz about MOVE IT! and Tabitha Fox. Rick Gallo is reconsidering his investment in the show, and the fans were very disappointed that you were not there tonight. Can you be there tomorrow night?

Yes, Hudson responded immediately. **I'll be there.** He couldn't bear the thought of the show suffering for any reason.

Thank you! Claudia wrote back. Hudson could practically sense the relief in her words. **Now get some rest! It's late already and you should be asleep!**

Yes, ma'am, Hudson wrote back. But despite his confidence—and his promise—he knew he had other work to do besides getting ready for the show. He opened the calendar on his phone. Today was Saturday. The cupcake competition was on Monday. *Our Time*, like many shows, didn't run on Mondays so the cast and crew could have a break.

Hudson immediately switched back to the group text with the Squad. **I'm going to perform tomorrow,** he wrote to his friends. **Claudia just texted and asked if I can.**

That's great! Monica wrote back. But before April or Relly could chime in, Hudson continued.

But I need your help, he wrote. **Can you come over really early tomorrow morning? Bring a big appetite.**

Fourteen

The next morning, Hudson was up before anyone else. His nani followed shortly.

"Hudson, you're up so early!" she exclaimed. "What are you doing?"

"I need to work on the cupcake recipe," he said. "And I need your help."

"But, Hudson, I need to make breakfast and then cook the big dinner we missed yesterday."

"The competition is tomorrow, and I'm not ready," Hudson insisted. "My friends are coming over soon to help."

"Okay, beta. I can help, and I'm glad your friends will be here too. We can work on dinner later. But what about breakfast?" his nani said. "The rest of the family will be up soon and will need to eat."

Hudson twisted his lip as he thought. He knew his parents both liked to have lazy Sundays at home to relax after the bustle of a busy week. But then he remembered their good mood from the night before.

"Maybe Mom and Dad would be up for going out," he said. "They could get bagels from H&H and then go to the Hungarian Pastry Shop. I remember Dad said they would visit a lot, years ago."

Hudson's grandmother glowed. "You certainly pay attention to the details in life. That's why you are so good with food."

Just then, the door buzzed.

"It's us!" It was Monica's voice in the speaker.

"Okay," Hudson said. "I'll let you in."

"Who was that?" Hudson's father asked as he wandered into the kitchen. "It's very early to have guests over."

"Your son has invited his friends from the theater over to help with the cupcake recipe. And he has planned a lovely morning for you and the rest of the family." Nani smiled and turned to Hudson.

"I hope it's okay that I invited the Squad over, but I'm running out of time," Hudson added. "The cupcake competition is tomorrow, and I haven't settled on a recipe. And

Claudia wants me back at the theater tonight."

He inhaled deeply. He didn't realize that he had been talking so quickly, so rushed, and had practically run out of breath.

"You've got a lot of work to do," his father said. "Of course you can have the kitchen this morning." Just then there was a knock on the door. "That must be your friends."

Hudson opened the door and let Relly, Monica, and April into the apartment.

"It's so good to see you!" April said, throwing her arms around Hudson. "We really needed you last night. I'm glad you will be back onstage tonight."

Hudson's father said hello to the group and was about to leave the kitchen when his mother-in-law stopped him.

She grinned brightly. "You haven't heard Hudson's plan for your morning with your wife and—" She broke off for a moment and turned back to Hudson. "Wait. Hudson, why don't we keep Sudhir and Nisha here again? Your father and mother can have some time together."

Hudson wasn't thrilled about the idea of his little brother hanging around the house—he knew Sudhir was starstruck by the rest of the Squad. Sudhir was in awe of Relly's dance moves, Monica's voice, and April's acting—and social media savvy. When the Squad was around, he was often lurking in the corners. And he had been overjoyed that they had come to the Diwali festival the day before.

But Hudson relented. The time alone would do his parents good.

"I think that's a great plan," he said. "And Sudhir can help as a taste-tester, too."

"No way!" his brother shouted. He was nowhere to be seen, but his voice was growing louder and louder as he walked toward the kitchen. "I'm always the guinea pig, and then you save the nice treats for your friends at the theater." He stopped short when he spotted the Squad. "Oh," he said, suddenly self-conscious in his shark-print pajamas. "I didn't know we had company."

"Go change," his father said. "I'll let your mother know that we have a . . . date." The mischief was evident in his eyes.

He started to walk out of the room but then turned back to Hudson.

"What did you plan for us?" he asked.

"Oh," Hudson began. "I didn't really plan anything exactly—"

"But he had such a lovely idea!" his nani interrupted.

"I just thought you could get bagels at H&H, maybe take them to Riverside Park to eat. And then you could go up to the Hungarian Pastry Shop by Columbia."

Hudson's father smiled. "That's *is* lovely idea, Hudson," he said. "I'll get your mother. You be a good host to your guests."

Over the next few hours, the kitchen was Hudson's kingdom. His friends had seen episodes of *Broadway Sizzlers* before, but they had never seen Hudson live in action. They were impressed by how adept he was in the kitchen.

Hudson started with the cupcake bases that he and his nani had begun working on the night before. He brought imli out from the refrigerator and piled spices on the counter.

"Spices?" Relly asked, confused. "What are you doing with spices for a cupcake recipe?"

"We're trying to figure that out," Hudson admitted. "Indian recipes are all about spice, so Nani suggested I try something with spice." He spotted the habaneros in the fridge and almost brought them out. But he changed his mind and left them where they were. *It needs more subtle spice,* he thought. *Maybe some cayenne?*

While the Squad—and Sudhir—munched on the cupcake bases from the night before, Nani pulled out the ingredients for badam barfi: sugar, rose water, cardamom powder, and almond flour.

"Just an idea," she said, shrugging as Hudson and his friends looked at her quizzically.

"It could go on top," Hudson said, understanding his nani's suggestion.

"On top, on the bottom, it's up to you," his nani said.

Hudson got to work. He made the badam barfi in less than forty-five minutes, with guidance from his nani, and had his friends taste it.

"That's really good," April said, taking a picture and posting it to Instagram.

Relly picked up a piece of red velvet cupcake with the badam barfi. He chewed it thoughtfully. Everyone watched him, waiting for the verdict. "Too much," he said. "The red velvet overpowers the nutty flavors."

"Look at you, becoming a true critic!" Nani teased. "That kind of feedback is helpful for the competition!"

"I'm just glad I'm not the only guinea pig this time," Sudhir said from the far end of the counter.

"The chocolate flavor also overpowers it," said Monica, who was seated at the table with Relly and April. She took a drink of water to clear her palate and then tried it with the plain vanilla cupcake.

"Now that, I like." She nodded animatedly as she took another bite. "But it's got to have more punch."

Hudson drizzled imli onto another vanilla cupcake and then placed a piece of the badam barfi on it. "How about that?" he asked. "Does it do anything to make it more interesting?"

Monica took a bite and reflected for a moment. "It does," she said. "Sweet again but also tangy." She cocked her head to the side. "I worry it would be overwhelming" It was a question more than a statement.

"That's an excellent observation!" Hudson's nani exclaimed.

Hudson was whipping up more sweets as they talked.

The base isn't right, he said to himself. *It needs more flavors.* He looked around the kitchen as his friends watched closely. "Cardamom," he said, adding some to the mix. "And . . . saffron!"

"Be careful with that," his nani whispered. "It's expensive."

Hudson suddenly stopped what he was doing and picked up his phone, which was sitting in a pile of flour. He was silent for a few moments, typing away and then reading carefully. Relly, Monica, and April looked at each other with wide eyes, wondering what he was up to. Nani just watched her grandson closely, leaning toward him from her seat by the counter.

Finally, Sudhir broke the silence. "What *is* it, Hudson?"

"I'm making gulab jamun," he said. "It's the same basic flavors—cardamom and saffron. Just no sticky syrup. Yet . . ."

"Don't worry about the syrup," his nani said, now up on

her feet. "You are on a good track. Keep going."

But a text message suddenly interrupted him. It was a group message to everyone in the Squad. They all picked up their phones and read it at the same time.

I need you all to get to the theater at once, Claudia had written. I know it's hardly 11, but Artie and I want to make sure everyone is in the best shape to perform. Drop what you are doing and get here immediately, please.

"I guess we have to go," Relly said, grabbing another chocolate cupcake. "Sorry we can't stay and help more."

"You haven't eaten anything proper yet!" Nani chided. "Let me make you something first, and then you can go to the theater."

"That's so kind of you," Monica said, "but we really should be going. When Claudia calls for us, it means we need to get there right away."

As the Squad got ready to leave, Nani gave Hudson a smile. "You are doing a good job. We'll figure the rest out before the competition," she said. "Don't worry." She turned to the mess in the kitchen. "And don't worry about all this. Sudhir and I will clean up before your parents get home. Just be sure to get some real food before you get to the theater."

Hudson gave his nani a long hug. "Thank you," he said, clearly frustrated that he had to leave in the middle of such a breakthrough with the recipe. But he had promised Claudia—and his friends—that he would be at the show. There wasn't time for everything today.

Hudson quickly washed his hands and threw his apron onto the counter. His friends were already leaving the apartment, and Nani was busy at the sink. He grabbed something from the fridge and tossed it in his backpack.

"Oh good, you're all here," Jimmy said when they arrived at the theater. "Claudia is as nervous as I've ever seen her, and Artie's pacing backstage. I don't think he can bear the stress."

The Squad moved quickly to the back of the theater, in search of Claudia. They found her at the entrance to the orchestra pit.

There was no time for a greeting. "Let's get to work. We have so much to do."

"Besides rehearse?" Hudson asked.

"Well, *Move It!* is all anyone can talk about, as you know, so we need to do some marketing. Maybe we can get some people to buy last-minute tickets."

"Last-minute tickets?" April said. "We've never had that problem before. She gave Claudia a worried look, but Claudia turned away without responding.

The Squad looked at each other. "We should go to TKTS in Duffy Square. You know, the place where the tourists buy discounted tickets? Get some interest there?" Monica suggested. "Abuelita and I picked up lots of tickets there when we first moved to New York. It's a great way to see shows for a good price."

"That's where all the *struggling* shows go to boost ticket sales," Relly said. "Well, mostly." He looked around quickly to make sure no one but the Squad could hear. "We should make sure *Our Time* is not on the board."

"TKTS is a great idea, kids," Claudia said. "We can encourage people to come to the box office to snap up the last seats for tonight's show. And Duffy Square is the heart of Times Square. You can get used to performing there. It's where the Fall Festival will be, and *Our Time* will be featured along with a few other shows."

"Yeah, we heard," April said. "*Move It!* will be one of them. We'll get to see Tabitha again."

Claudia ignored April's sarcasm. "April, be sure to get it on *all* the social channels. Your TikTok videos have been doing really well." She suddenly became very thoughtful. "Actually," she said, "how about I come with you and take the pictures and videos? I don't know anything about those social channels, but that way you'll all be in them."

"Great idea!" April said excitedly.

The Squad dropped their bags off in their dressing rooms. Before they left, Hudson went back to the one he shared with Relly. But he noticed something was missing.

"Where's my hot plate?" he wondered aloud. He kept it in the dressing room to heat up food before the show and sometimes at intermission, but he had not used it in quite some time. He opened a cabinet door that was filled with snacks and costume scraps. "There it is!" he said, pulling it out from behind a box of crackers. He set it to the side just as Relly burst back into the room. "Come on, Hudson, we can't let you disappoint the fans again."

The Squad made the short walk to Times Square. The fall weather was unpredictable, and the temperature had dropped a bit from the day before.

The line at the TKTS booth was long.

"Let's set up there, in the middle of the square. Everyone in the line will be able to see us," April said. "And there will be enough space for Claudia to film properly."

Hudson snuck away for a moment to look at the list of shows on the TKTS board. *Our Time* was not on it. He ran back to join the Squad. Monica, Relly, and Hudson looked relieved to see him shake his head no and flash a thumbs-up.

The Squad stretched gently as they decided what to do. "Let's sing," Monica suggested. She started. *"Look, Ma, I finally made it . . ."* April, Relly, and Hudson jumped in, while Claudia stood back to get them all in the shot. People in line at the TKTS booth stopped talking and turned to watch the group. When the Squad had finished their song, they approached the line, where a man was beckoning them closer.

"What song was that?" the man asked. He had a gruff Boston accent. "It was beautiful."

"It's called 'Mama.' It's from the show we're in, *Our Time,*" Monica said. "There are tickets available for tonight's show," she added.

"You kids are in a show?" the man asked. "You're too young for that kind of thing."

"Nothing's impossible in New York City, especially not on Broadway," Relly said.

The man gave the kids a good look. "We were planning to see an off-Broadway play tonight, but maybe we should see your show instead. What do you think, honey?" he asked, turning to his wife.

"We can see which show has better seats tonight and then see the other later this week," his wife said. "Thanks, kids."

The Squad was heartened by the good response. April, who had been helping Claudia upload the video to TikTok, joined her friends. "Maybe one more song? Or we could simply dance? Maybe do a TikTok challenge video? Those get attention."

"Better you than me trying to figure out those TikTok videos," Claudia said, laughing. "But that could help show your real selves, not just your characters."

The man with the Boston accent motioned for Relly to come back. "Do you know anything about a show called *Move It!?*" he asked. "I keep hearing all about it, but I don't see it on the board here."

Relly was crestfallen. "That show hasn't opened yet," he explained. "They're still in rehearsals." He paused before walking away. "Just remember, sir, when you get tickets for *Our Time*, you'll have to go directly to the box office at the Ethel Merman Theater. You won't find them here at the TKTS booth."

"What was that about?" April asked when Relly rejoined the group.

"Oh, he just wanted to know where to get tickets to *Our Time*," Relly said. "How about one TikTok challenge, and then we go somewhere else?"

"Let's skip the challenge," Hudson said. "How about we just let the audience know where we are and what we're up to?"

"Now, *that* sounds like an IG Live," April said. "So many platforms, so little time!"

The Squad took turns in front of the camera. They made sure to show off the glittering Times Square lights and then sang a few bars of another *Our Time* song.

All of a sudden, the lights of a giant video screen caught their eye. It was a large-than-life photo of Tabitha. *Tabitha Fox, the original star of* Our Time, *will tell* Good Morning America *about the "curse" of the Ethel Merman Theater and why she backed out of the show,* the caption read. *Catch her on Broadway soon as the lead in* Move It!

Monica, Relly, Hudson and April all stared at the screen. Their mouths hung open in shock.

"What could she possibly say?" Monica was exasperated. "Why can't she move on? She's doing great work. Why does she have to pick on us?"

"Why don't you kids chat up more people in the TKTS line?" Claudia interrupted. She had seen the ad too but chose to ignore it. "They seem to respond to personal interaction. And tell them you're available for autographs if they want them and that they can see you onstage, under the bright lights of the Ethel Merman."

The Squad spent the next half hour doing just what Claudia had suggested. They managed to convince several people to buy tickets to their show, mostly families with children who were impressed that kids their own age were already Broadway stars. They posed for photographs, gave out autographs, and sang one more song before heading back to the theater.

"Everything okay?" Hudson asked Monica on the way back.

"Yes, I'm good," Monica said. "That's just really exhausting. I can't wait to get back to the theater to rest for a bit. And Tabitha is aggravating." She waved her hand to dismiss Tabitha from her thoughts. Then she looked at Hudson carefully. "How about you? Are you okay?"

"I'm tired," Hudson said. He let out a big, loud yawn and stretched.

"Is that all?" Monica asked, leaning closer and raising an eyebrow at her friend.

Hudson was clearly distracted, and he knew he couldn't hide anything from his friend. "I just have an idea for the cupcake."

"That's great!" Monica said, genuinely happy for Hudson. "But let's focus on the show first. We've got to nail it tonight."

"I'll do my best," he said. "I promise."

Back at the Ethel Merman, the Squad collapsed into chairs in the main theater. "I could use a nap," April said.

"Me too," Relly said. "And a snack."

"What do you kids need?" It was Jimmy Onions, a green apple in hand. "I can get you something if you're hungry.

And you know you can always sleep in the dressing rooms. You have time before the big show tonight—unless Claudia and Artie want you to rehearse."

"They can rest for a bit before the show." Artie's voice came loud and clear from the front of the theater. "No one is ever going to perform well if they haven't gotten enough rest. Right, Hudson?"

Everyone turned to Hudson, who was clearly lost in his own world.

"Hudson?" April said.

"What?" Hudson said. "Oh, rest. Yes, everyone needs to rest." He got up and stretched again. "I'm going to rest right now." He headed toward his dressing room.

On the way, he ran into Jacob.

"Hi, Hudson!" the younger boy said enthusiastically. "Good to see you! I hope you are feeling better. I had a great time performing last night!" Hudson could tell Jacob was limping a bit.

"I'm glad to hear it," Hudson said. "But are you okay? I heard you took a tumble afterward and banged up your knee pretty bad."

Jacob blushed. "I did," he said, pulling up his pant leg to show the damage. A large bandage covered his knee. "Wanna see?" he asked, pulling the bandage away. "It's starting to change colors!"

"No, thanks!" Hudson said forcefully. The thought of what it might look like made him squeamish. "I hope it feels better," he said. "But I've got to rest before the show."

He pushed past Jacob and stepped into the dressing room, closing the door behind him. Once alone, he turned to his hot plate, picking up the pan and examining it closely, making sure it was clean. He opened the cabinet door again and pulled out the large bottle of olive oil, a bottle of balsamic vinegar, and a box of salt he kept there. From his backpack he pulled out the pre-chopped yellow onions he had dropped in there just as he and his friends were getting ready to leave his family's house earlier that day. He plugged in the hot plate and turned it on.

He scrolled through his phone to double-check his method for caramelizing onions. After a few moments of the hot plate heating, he sprinkled some water from his water bottle to see if it would bubble up. It did—the plate was ready for the olive oil, which Hudson poured on. Once satisfied that the oil was hot enough, he started to pour in the onions but then stopped himself.

Maybe I should be filming this for Broadway Sizzlers, he suddenly thought. *Or for social media. "Behind the scenes at the theater." April would love that.* He checked the clock on his phone to make sure he had enough time to start over and film before the show. He also checked to make sure he had enough ingredients left. He had plenty of both. His usual camera equipment was at home, but he could always use his smartphone. He looked around the dressing room for something suitable to hold it up but came up empty. He quietly opened the dressing room door and peered out into the hallway to see if the coast was clear. A voice caught him by surprise.

"What's up, Hudson?" It was Jimmy.

"You scared me!" Hudson said, his eyes wide. He stood up straight again, almost as tall as Jimmy. "I'm just looking for something to hold my camera while I shoot a video."

"Solo?" Jimmy said. "I thought you were all shooting those social media videos together, for Instagram and TikTok."

Hudson thought he caught a bit of suspicion in the doorman's eye, but then Jimmy simply shrugged.

"Follow me," Jimmy said. "I think I have some things that might help."

He turned, and Hudson followed him down the corridor to a room Hudson had never noticed before. He watched quietly as Jimmy rummaged through technical equipment. "How about this?" he asked, holding up a portable camera tripod. "April left it behind one day. I think it's perfectly functional—it's just missing a remote. April thought it was useless to her. But I think it will do the trick for you." He handed the stand to Hudson.

"This is perfect! Thanks, Jimmy," Hudson said. Jimmy led the way out of the room and back toward the dressing rooms. He took only a few steps before stopping short. He turned his nose up to the air and sniffed several times.

"Is something burning?" he asked.

"Don't say it, Jimmy." It was Artie, who suddenly flew out of his office. "You know you can't yell fire in a crowded theater!"

"Well, good thing the theater isn't crowded yet," Jimmy said, following his nose down the hall, Artie and Hudson trailing him closely.

"And remember the last time there was a fire in here—the sprinkler system caused the waterfall to collapse! And the theater nearly flooded!" Artie was nearly out of breath.

Jimmy found himself right outside Hudson and Relly's dressing room. He pushed open the door and immediately spotted the hot plate, where the few slices of onions Hudson had left in the oil were starting to burn. It took just a few strides to cross the room and reach the hot plate. He unplugged it and removed the pan.

"No fire, Artie," Jimmy said. "Just a little smoke."

Both men turned to Hudson, who desperately wanted to disappear.

"Hudson, you can't leave a hot plate on in the dressing room," Artie began.

"I'm sorry," Hudson said. "I know better than to do that. I got distracted looking for something to hold my camera. . . ." He stopped himself from explaining further, knowing that he had made a huge mistake.

"What's going on?" It was Relly. Hudson, Artie, and Jimmy turned to him, with April and Monica close behind.

"Hudson, the food is here," Relly said, then wrinkled his nose. "Is that smoke?"

"Is there a fire?" April shouted.

"No, there's no fire," Artie said, gesticulating wildly to calm April down. "Just a little accident with a hot plate that got a little too . . . hot," he said.

Now the entire Squad turned to Hudson. "What happened, Hudson?" Monica asked.

Hudson closed his eyes, again wishing he could just disappear. He thought maybe he could tell his friends that he was working on a treat for them, that maybe that would soften the blow of the mistake he had made leaving the hot plate unattended.

"I was trying to caramelize some onions," he said instead, opting for the truth. "I walked away for a few minutes to look for something, and they burned."

"Was it for the cupcake? For your recipe for the competition?" Monica asked quietly.

Hudson nodded, looking down at his feet, feeling he had let his friends down.

Jimmy broke the silence. "Let's get rid of the hot plate, Hudson," he said. "And I'll bring a fan in here to clear out the smoke."

Artie shuffled out, and Jimmy put a comforting hand on Hudson's shoulder for a moment. "It's okay, Hudson," he said. "No one got hurt, and that's what matters most."

Jimmy left the room. An awkward silence fell upon Hudson, Monica, Relly, and April.

"I'm sorry," Hudson said glumly. "I just really want to win that competition,"

"We've got to focus on the show tonight, though," Relly said. "Wait—you were making onions for . . . the *cupcake*?"

Hudson nodded. "Yeah, I wanted to try it to see if it would make a decent garnish."

"No—no onions," Relly said. April also grimaced at the thought of onions—even caramelized ones—on a cupcake.

"Shall we eat?" Monica asked. "The sandwiches Jimmy ordered are here."

"I'm not hungry," Hudson said immediately. "I'm going to take a walk." He saw the surprised, concerned looks on his friends' faces. "I just need to clear my head." He left the room without another word.

While he was gone, Hudson realized he was indeed hungry. He stopped at Black Tap for a Truffle Hot Honey Chicken Sandwich. He considered ordering one of their famous—albeit over-the-top—milkshakes, but it would have been too much sugar, especially for one person. He thought it would be nice to get some doughnuts for the Squad and the rest of the people at the theater. His first thought was to head to Peter Pan Donuts in Greenpoint, but after checking the time again, he knew he wouldn't have enough time to get all the way to Brooklyn and back before the show. He considered going to Balthazar Bakery for petit fours, but when he exited the train near the Flatiron Building, he realized he had forgotten all about Dough, another doughnut shop he adored. He picked up an assortment, choosing a hibiscus doughnut—his favorite—for himself.

When he got back to the Ethel Merman, he quickly put on his costume before seeking out the rest of the Squad. April, Relly, and Monica were already in costume and warmed up. They were about to give an Instagram Live "backstage tour" of the theater.

"Come join us, Hudson!" April said excitedly.

But Relly lost interest in the tour when he spotted the box in Hudson's hand.

"Are those doughnuts?" Relly asked. "From Dough?"

"Yes, they are," Hudson said, opening the box for his friends. "Hands off the hibiscus one, though. That's mine."

"Let's save those for intermission," Monica said. "Or even after the show."

"Take your pick now, though, or the crew may eat them all," Hudson said.

They got paper towels and placed their selections on them, leaving the doughnuts in their dressing rooms. Hudson quickly changed and did a few quick stretches to help loosen up before the show.

"Okay, let's tell Instagram our favorite things about the Ethel Merman," April said, starting to film.

"I love the dressing rooms," Relly said. "They're cozy and they have all my stuff."

"I like the statue of Ethel Merman," Monica said. She did, after all, have a special connection to it.

"I like the stage, especially when I'm under the lights!" April said, turning the camera to herself. "Hudson, what about you?"

Hudson was quiet. "Hudson, what's your favorite part of the theater?" April said again, this time poking him with her foot.

"I like the people," Hudson mumbled.

"What's that?" April asked. "I couldn't hear you."

"The people," Hudson said, louder this time. "The people are the best thing about the theater." His gaze drifted away from the camera, his thoughts somewhere else again. "I'll be right back," he said. "I need to write something down."

"All right, then," April said, still filming, trying to save the Instagram Live. "Let's go on a tour."

In his dressing room, Hudson found some paper and a pen in his backpack and started writing. *Gulab jamun base, imli for a bit of a tangy taste, a layer of barfi. Maybe more than one flavor of barfi?* He started listing the different colors of barfi that he normally saw. *Pink and green, or plain white for the almond type.*

Claudia interrupted his thoughts. "Hudson, it's showtime!" she chirped. "Why aren't you with the others?"

"I just had to get a few things on paper before I forgot," he said.

"Okay, well, places!"

Hudson joined the rest of the Squad onstage. He could tell they—especially April—were annoyed by him leaving them in the middle of a show promotion.

But they made it through the show without major incident—no tripping onstage, no landing in the waterfall, no one singing off-key. Relly's dance moves made the crowd swoon, and Monica's singing captivated them. April's sudden enthusiasm had them laughing. Hudson felt like he was just there as support, that he wasn't adding anything special.

"These are so pretty," Monica said during intermission as she and the rest of the Squad nibbled on their doughnuts. "I almost don't want to eat it."

So, presentation really does matter, Hudson thought. *Just like Dad always says.*

Before they knew it, Claudia was back, ushering them to the stage for act two. After the show, they went through their usual routine, but for Hudson, signing autographs had lost its magic.

As soon as they finished, April started talking about Tabitha and her upcoming *Good Morning America* interview. "When is it airing?" She was scrolling through her phone for information.

"Forget about Tabitha and *Move It!*" Hudson exploded. "We are as good as we are ever going to be. If they are better, and if the crowds love Tabitha and kids dressed as cute animals, well, that's the way it will have to be. I have to get through the cupcake competition!"

The Squad was shocked into silence.

"You have to focus." April was the first to speak, standing on her toes, defiant.

Hudson stared at her. "I've got to get through the cupcake competition. It's tomorrow. And I don't know if Broadway is my main dream."

Relly, April, and Monica were speechless. For them, starring in *Our Time* was hopefully just the beginning of long careers onstage.

"How can you say such a thing, Hudson?" April shouted. "This dream is *all* of our dream. We're in this show together."

"Yeah, Hudson, what kind of friend would say such a thing? You're part of this squad too," Relly added.

Hudson was already grabbing his backpack to leave. "If I have to choose, I've told you already: right now, I need to win this cupcake competition."

Monica had been silent up until now, and she was near tears. As she and the others watched Hudson storm off, she finally spoke. "He has to decide for himself what's right. He has to follow his dreams—just like I did."

Fifteen

The closer Hudson got to home, the worse he felt for getting upset with his friends. *I have to apologize,* he thought.

As soon as he entered the apartment, he headed toward his bedroom so he could call his friends. But his plans changed when he ran into his nani in the living room.

"I think I have the flavors of the cupcake figured out," he said. "But I'm worried about the construction."

"Okay," his nani said. "Let's get to it."

"Oh," Hudson added, "and it really does need some spice. Maybe cayenne? Or paprika? Garam masala?"

Over the next few hours, the two worked on recipes, pairing everything with a spice. Mango and then raspberry with paprika. Nuts with garam masala. A mix of all together. Whatever they tried, Hudson was convinced that something more was necessary—he just wasn't sure what it was. In the middle of it all, he had whipped up fresh gulab jamun cupcakes, this time adding a bit of mango and paprika.

"Tell me about the judge," his grandmother said as they worked together. "Who is Charlie Richards?"

Hudson wasn't sure what his grandmother was getting at. "He's just a guy from Colorado who made it big with a FoodTube show."

"Tell me more. Give me details. You have to pay attention to the details and know who your audience is, you know."

Hudson took a drink of water and popped a cracker into his mouth to clear his palate. He took a seat next to his nani at the kitchen table.

"He's a cowboy from western Colorado."

"Is he a real cowboy?" His grandmother was excited. "I love cowboys. I watched a lot of Westerns when I was growing up in India."

Hudson shared what he knew of Charlie's story. "His father and grandfather were ranchers and opened a restaurant. Charlie got into the family business and then left the area for school. He kept working in restaurants, though, and experimented with all sorts of food. Ultimately, he found fame on FoodTube."

"So he adapted the cowboy persona for the show?" his grandmother asked.

"It's part of his roots, but he brought it back for the show. It makes him unique."

It was true—Charlie wasn't like other people on the channel, most of whom were professionally trained chefs or had perfect kitchens. What people liked about Charlie was his approachability: he was a guy with a grill, and his only formal training came from working not only in his family's restaurant but also in barbecue restaurants and pizza joints. His curiosity about regular people's kitchens and raw reality made him famous.

"So," Nani said, bringing him back to the matter at hand. "How do we really get his attention?"

Hudson pursed his lips. "I think you figured that out a long time ago. With chilis."

His nani gave a hearty laugh. "You caught me! I've been watching his videos. And yes, he likes spicy food. Really hot stuff."

The timer on the oven went off, and Hudson pulled the fresh cupcake bases out of the oven. The sounds from the kitchen had woken Hudson's father, who had fallen asleep while reading a book in the living room. The smells lured him into the room.

"What's this?" he asked, walking directly to the cupcakes. "It smells very good."

"Thanks, Dad," Hudson said. "It's basically a gulab jamun without the sticky syrup. I mixed in mango and paprika."

"May I try one?" his father asked, already reaching for the tray.

"Sure, but just one. We need to play with the rest to make sure the construction is okay. I think I have an idea for the flavors, but I don't know how to make it work physically."

"Come with me, Hudson," his father said, grabbing his coat instead of a cupcake. "Get your jacket. You can come, too, if you'd like," he said to his mother-in-law.

The three left the apartment building and started walking down Riverside Drive. "First things first, Hudson," his father said. "Stand up straight. You're always slumping, unless you're onstage or you are in the kitchen. It looks like you are always trying to hide from something."

Hudson took his hands out of his pockets and relaxed his shoulders away from his ears. In just a few steps, he was feeling better, more confident. His father noticed and patted him on the back. "Good, beta," he said.

"Look up," his father said. "Look at the unique details on the buildings. Some of them have been here for over a hundred years. But you'll miss it all if you are looking down at your feet."

The trio stopped and looked up. They had made it to the historic section of Riverside Drive at Eightieth and Eighty-First Streets. "Wow," Hudson said, noticing the ornate decoration above the entryway of the building before them.

"That's Elizabethan Renaissance Revival style," his father rattled off.

"It's like a giant castle," Hudson said, stepping back to look at the building as a whole. "I can't believe I've never noticed it before."

"It's easy to overlook the things you are surrounded by all the time," his dad said. "Sometimes you have to slow down and step back to appreciate them."

Hudson was still admiring the ornate details on the building. "There's one thing I can't get over," he said, turning to his father. "Making a mistake. I've made so many mistakes in *Our Time* lately, and I'm not sure I can handle a big mistake here with the cupcake competition."

Hudson's father, normally jovial, was very serious now. "Hudson, beta," he began, "do you know how long it takes to become an architect? Eight years. At least. And think about your mother's medical studies. It took her eight years just to do the basics. Her fellowships have taken even more time. Becoming an expert takes time, and even then everyone makes mistakes. The point is that you have to learn from them."

"It's true, Hudson," Nani added. "No one is perfect. Mistakes happen. But you do your absolute best to correct the mistakes as soon as you discover them."

A biting breeze enveloped them. They all shuddered, particularly Hudson's nani, who had only grabbed a light-weight Kashmiri shawl on her way out the door. Noticing her discomfort, Hudson said, "Let's go back."

"Is there anything that may have inspired you over the past few days that would be fitting for the design of the cupcake you're creating?" Nani asked as they waited for the elevator back up to the apartment.

Hudson pulled out his phone and started scrolling through the pictures he had taken at the Diwali party the day before. There was an explosion of color—the tasty food, the stunning decorations, and the intricate outfits. He felt a tinge of sadness when he got to a selfie he had taken with April, Monica, and Relly, Sudhir photobombing in the background. He paused there, thinking he really should call each of his friends. But now he was afraid they wouldn't want to talk to him after his outburst earlier.

He scrolled through a few more pictures, then landed on one that caught his eye. It was of five women dancing, their heads topped with decorations that looked like tall towers of baskets or jugs. They balanced these decorations easily, often without even using their hands, as they danced.

"This." Hudson showed the picture to his nani, then to his father. "This is what it needs to look like. As much as possible."

"Ah, those are special costumes for Gujarati folk dances," his nani said brightly. "I have worn those before. It's challenging to learn how to balance them, but once you've got it, it's a lot of fun!"

"I'll tell you this," Hudson's father chimed in. "That may be difficult to replicate as a cupcake, to make it balance properly. But see how you can improvise. Just like you and your friends do onstage sometimes."

Once back inside the apartment, Hudson's father, now wide awake, headed back to the living room to continue reading, while Hudson and his nani started working away again in the kitchen.

After another hour, they were convinced they had it right—almost. Cardamom, saffron, mango, a hint of pistachio, a drizzle of imli, and a special ingredient—chili powder.

"Now, to assemble it," Hudson said. He stared at all

the different pieces he wanted to include: the gulab jamun (without all the sticky syrup), the rose barfi, the pista barfi, and the imli. "The gulab jamun will be the base," he said, placing one in front of him on a cutting board. He wasn't sure what to do next. "Maybe a layer of imli to hold the rose barfi and pista barfi in place?" He spread a thick layer of imli on the base and then placed the two types of barfi next. First he set them next to each other, but they were too large and falling off. Next he he tried placing the pista barfi first before topping it off with the rose barfi, the silver leaf shining on top. "That's not very interesting," he said, turning toward Nani. "It's just a big stack. And it doesn't look anything like the decorative headpieces we saw at the Diwali festival."

Nani thought for a moment. "What if you had multiple layers of the gulab jamun?" she offered. "And different barfi in between."

"I like that!" Hudson said. "But that will make it bigger—and it can't be too big or you won't get all the flavors together when you bite into it."

Another hour went by to make sure the flavors were in the right order—and that the structure didn't topple over.

"I think it needs to be bigger at the base," his nani suggested gently at one point. She had spotted Hudson's father peering around the corner into the kitchen. He was curious about their progress but did not want to interrupt, especially at this stage of the game. He had, however, gestured to his mother-in-law that the base was too small.

"You're right," Hudson said. "At this size, it will never hold up." His dad gave his nani a big smile and a thumbs-up. The smells from the kitchen had now woken Hudson's mother, who was eager for a late-night snack. She joined her husband and watched for a moment, resting her head on her husband's shoulder, glad that her son was looking the happiest he had been in a long time.

While his parents retreated to the living room, Hudson put the final piece on the cupcake, eager to make sure it would stand. It was a layer of rose-colored barfi, complete with edible silver leaf paper.

Hudson took a moment to look over what he had built: At the base was gulab jamun, followed by a layer of pista barfi. It was pliable, and Hudson had molded it just so to help hold the next layer of gulab jamun in place. On top of that third layer, he had spread mango shrikhand, a yogurt-based dessert to which he had added a heavy dose of paprika. Then there was another layer of gulab jamun, followed by a piece of rose barfi, complete with the edible silver leaf and drizzled with imli.

Hudson carefully picked it up. "Okay," he said, turning to his grandmother. "Do you want to try it?"

"Shouldn't the baker always be the first to taste his creation?" Nani asked.

Hudson nodded. "You're right," he said. He picked up the cupcake, which was much larger than a regular cupcake might be, given all the layers. He had to open his mouth as wide as possible to get all the flavors together.

Hudson closed his eyes as he chewed, then opened them, staring off into the corner of the kitchen, his bangs falling into his eyes. He closed his eyes yet again, this time shutting them really tight. Once he swallowed, he opened his eyes again, but he just stared at the remainder of the cupcake.

"Well?" his grandmother asked. "How is it?"

"It's missing something," he said. "I like all the flavors, and I love the way it looks. But maybe it needs more heat. To balance out all the sweet, you know?"

"Should you sprinkle on some chili powder?" Nani asked, picking up the bottle and looking at the label. "Or do you need a hotter kind?"

"Dad has the really hot kind in the cabinet, I think," Hudson said, rummaging through it.

He found the container and tasted a bit to see just how hot it was. "That's better," he said, "but I'm not sure it will be enough."

He dusted a fair amount of the chili powder onto the cupcake and then took another big bite.

"Yeah," he said, still chewing. "It's better, but I don't think it's quite enough." He pushed the cupcake toward his grandmother. "Here, Nani, you try."

His nani couldn't hide her excitement. "I'm so excited to try the cupcake," she said. "I'm very proud of you, Hudson."

Hudson raised an eyebrow as he pushed his bangs away from his eyes. "But you haven't tasted it yet!"

"I'm still very proud of you," she said, rocking her head from side to side as she picked up the cupcake. "You tried something new, and you *made* something new. It takes courage to let your creative projects into the world."

With that, she took as big a bite of the cupcake as she could. She just barely managed to get all the flavors. Hudson watched her curiously as she chewed, her eyes also closed. Once she finished, she took in a long breath.

"I think it's great," she said. "But is it enough for your judge, Charlie Richards?"

Hudson took a long moment to reflect on what his nani was saying. His parents, who had been listening to the conversation from the living room, peeked into the kitchen again.

"May we come in?" his mother asked delicately. Her stomach was now growling.

"Ajo, ajo," Nani said. "Come, come. Help us decide if the cupcake is finished or not."

Hudson started assembling two more cupcakes, one for each of his parents. Once ready, he placed one before his mother and another before his father.

"Wait!" he exclaimed just as they were about to pick them up. "The extra-hot chili powder! You have to try it with that." Hudson reached for the container of his father's favorite hot chili powder and sprinkled it on with a flourish.

"That's a nice touch, Hudson," his mother said, "adding the final ingredient in front of your customers."

With that, she picked up her cupcake. It took her two bites to get all the flavors. Her husband waited for her to start chewing before picking up his own. Hudson and his nani watched the two intently as they took their time analyzing the flavors.

"It's very good," his mother said. "I like the way you added the mango and used the gulab jamun as a base but without all the sticky syrup. And the imli drizzle is a nice touch."

"Yes, Hudson, it's excellent," his father added. "But I have to say, I don't really notice the chili powder."

"That's because your taste buds have been burned off with all the hot chilis you eat," his mother teased, nudging her husband with her hand.

"Well, that may be," Nani said, "but it seems that the judge Charlie Richards also has lost his taste buds, from what I know. He also loves very hot chilis."

"So what can I do?" Hudson was exasperated. "I need something hotter, but I don't know where to find it."

His nani didn't miss a beat. "Hudson, you have to go to Queens. That's where all the flavors are. The hot ones, in particular."

"But where exactly? The competition is tomorrow night at six."

"There's a family that owns a few grocery stores, but one of them is exclusively for spices. They have everything, including all the chilis you could want. The wife runs the place, while her husband drives a taxi—"

"Wait a minute," Hudson interrupted. "You're talking about G.G.!"

"G.G.?" Nani said, looking at him quizzically.

Hudson ran to his backpack, emptying everything before he found Gian Singh Giani's card at the bottom. "Here," he said. "He gave my friends and me a ride home from Kalustyan's in his taxi. He said he is a fan of *Broadway Sizzlers*, and he didn't charge us for the ride. He said I could call him G.G."

"That must be him," Hudson's nani said. "You'll have to

find him. And ask him if he has that pepper I asked you to buy the other day."

Hudson's parents had sat quietly, listening to the conversation as they finished their cupcakes.

"Will you have time?" Hudson's dad finally asked. "As you said, the competition is tomorrow, and it always takes a lot of time to navigate Queens."

Hudson suddenly felt very nervous. "I'll need help," he admitted. He turned to his nani. "You know where the stores are. Will you come with me?"

His nani giggled for a moment and then got very serious. "I'd love to, Hudson," she said. "But I'll only slow you down. These old knees, you know."

"You always say that," Hudson's mom said. "You're saving them for your dancing practice."

Nani frowned. "I am not quite the adventurer I once was." She hopped off her stool and put both hands on Hudson's shoulders. "Why don't you take your friends?" She winked. "*They* are adventurers, I know."

Sixteen

Back in his bedroom, Hudson was careful not to wake Sudhir, who had fallen asleep with a comic book in his hands again. He gently removed his brother's glasses and placed them in their case on the desk before turning off the light.

It was nearly three a.m. Hudson sat on the edge of his bed and stared at his phone. He was surprised for a moment to see that there were no messages—neither April, Relly, nor Monica had reached out, even though hours had gone by since their big blowout at the Ethel Merman.

Hudson sighed and ran a hand through his hair. He quietly kicked off his shoes and got into bed, not bothering to change into pajamas. He was incredibly tired, but he kept thinking about his friends. If it hadn't been the middle of the night, he would have texted.

"First thing in the morning," Hudson said. "I'll call each of them first thing in the morning."

And with that he fell asleep.

The alarm went off at seven o'clock the next morning, but Hudson was so tired that instead of hitting snooze, he inadvertently turned off the alarm. He didn't wake up again until ten a.m. It was the most sleep he had gotten in many days.

But when he woke up, he was very disoriented. He knew it was Monday, the day Broadway rested—there were no *Our Time* shows today. He didn't have to rush to the theater. It took him a few moments to recall that it was the day of the big cupcake competition.

"I have to get the final ingredient!" he shouted.

He spotted his phone on the nightstand and remembered that he had intended to personally call each of his friends. Looking at the clock, he wasn't sure he'd be able to do so. But he thought he had to try. He picked up his phone and looked for messages, but just as the night before, there weren't any.

Hudson hesitated for a moment and then decided to start with Monica.

"Hello?" she said, when she answered. "Hudson, I'm on the train, so I might lose you if we go underground."

"I'm really, truly sorry about last night," Hudson began. "I really value your friendship and the rest of the Squad's. And I'm sorry . . ."

"Hudson, you're breaking up," Monica said. "I'm meeting Relly and April at the Ethel Merman. Join us there." With that, the line went dead.

He thought about calling Relly and April, too, but then realized they must also be on their way to the theater and probably couldn't answer. He glanced at the clock again and saw that time was running short.

"They may be upset, but Monica wouldn't ask me to join them if she didn't think we could make up." Hudson ran to the bathroom to wash up. He was still wearing the same clothes as the night before.

He quickly showered and brushed his teeth and then threw on whatever clothes he could find: a long-sleeved black shirt, gray pants, and gray sneakers. The competition was scheduled to start at six p.m. He pulled up the email from Charlie Richards that had announced he was a finalist and watched the video again. What had Charlie said? Bring your own ingredients. The organizers will supply the tools and general ingredients like milk, eggs, and flour. Send a list of the ingredients you will be using in the morning.

Hudson slowly wrote out a list of the ingredients, packing his backpack as he went—he couldn't afford to forget anything. It was filled to the brim with mango, saffron, the silver leaf paper, and more. He typed the list into an email. "What about the chili?" Hudson said aloud. He thought carefully for a moment, unsure of what to write. *A very special ingredient—a chili,* he finally wrote. Per the instructions, he submitted a list of who would be coming to watch—his parents, his brother and baby sister, his nani. He hesitated a moment. Would his friends still want to come after what had happened last night? He took a deep breath and added April, Monica, and Relly to the list. Then he hit send.

Hudson was about to head out the door when he remembered to grab G.G.'s card. It was still sitting on the kitchen counter, where he had left it the night before.

"I'm going to need this," he said, slipping it into his jacket pocket and then locking the door to the empty apartment behind him.

Hudson was breathless when he arrived at the theater. He had just missed the train and had to wait longer than he liked for the next one. April, Relly, and Monica were waiting for him outside the stage door. They stood in a tight circle and hardly made room for him to join them.

Hudson looked at each of his friends carefully. "I'm

sorry about last night," he blurted out. "I don't want to fight. . . ."

"Just catch your breath, buddy," Relly said without turning to look at Hudson. April wouldn't look at him either.

Hudson took several deep breaths.

"I'm really sorry," he started again, more calmly this time. "I was going to call each of you early this morning to apologize, but I overslept. Your friendship means a lot to me. More than the show, more than the cupcake competition. I don't want to fight."

"The show is incredibly important." April finally looked up at him. "But so is the cupcake competition."

Hudson was speechless.

Relly patted him on the back. "We want you to win too, Hudson," he said.

"Well," Hudson said, "I want you to come to the competition. Not only that, but I'd really love it if you could help me beforehand." Monica, Relly, and April were all now looking at him curiously. No one said anything, so Hudson continued. "I need you to come to Queens with me. Consider it an adventure, a quest for the final missing ingredient."

"Ooh, an adventure!" April squealed. "I love an adventure!"

"Do you have time?" Monica asked, glancing at her phone. "It's nearly noon!"

"That's why I need your help. I need an extra set of tasters to get through it all quickly."

"We were planning to go to Katz's Deli for lunch. I'm craving a Reuben sandwich," Relly said.

"They have the best potato latkes. And great matzo ball soup," Hudson said. "But if it's okay with you, that will all have to wait."

"All right," Relly said. "But we should get going. Good thing we don't have a show today."

The friends headed off to the train. "Where in Queens are we going exactly?" Relly asked. He knew the city best, especially the outer boroughs, and was already plotting the route in his head.

"Jackson Heights," Hudson said. "We've got to find G.G., the taxi driver who drove us home on Diwali. The one who gave me his card."

"How can he help?" Monica asked, confused.

"His family has some small grocery stores. And one of the stores is exclusively for spices and chilis. Hot ones."

"Hot spices?" April was incredulous. "For a cupcake?"

The Squad had arrived at the train station. While waiting for the one that would take them to Queens, Hudson explained to his friends how his grandmother had convinced him that he needed to create something that would catch Charlie Richards's attention—and be accessible to a variety of palates. "My grandmother thinks G.G. can help," Hudson said.

"Well, let's see what we can find," Monica said as they got on the train.

On the way, April rattled off facts about the borough, known as a "Melting Pot."

"Astoria has a huge Greek population," she explained to Monica as she showed her a map on her phone. "And Woodside has large Irish and Filipino communities. Corona is Mexican, and Flushing is Chinese. The Far Rockaways have great Italian restaurants."

Hudson wasn't listening. He got impatient when the train got held up for fifteen minutes between stations, just before their last stop. No explanation for the delay was given, but there was no time for delays today. Hudson looked at the time on his phone. It was already one thirty p.m.

"Finally!" Hudson exclaimed as he and his friends tumbled out of the station and onto the street. "Now we just have to find G.G." He pulled G.G.'s card out of his pocket, looking for an address. But it didn't list one. He tried calling the number on the card. The phone rang several times, but it never went to voicemail, and no one picked up.

"No answer," he said, now nervous.

"What does the card say?" Relly asked, suspicious.

"It just says, 'Sajna's Specialty Spice Shop,'" Hudson said.

"Well, let's ask someone," April said, approaching the first person she saw, a middle-aged woman in a honey-colored salwar kameez with a heavy maroon shawl draped over her shoulders. "Excuse me, do you know where Sajna's shop is?"

"Which one?" the woman asked.

"Well, the one with all the chilis, I think," April said, unusually unsure of herself.

The woman narrowed her eyes at April, pulling her shawl closer as the wind suddenly picked up. An overhead train rumbled loudly nearby. Without a word, the woman responded simply by pointing down the street.

"It's that way," April said, turning back to the Squad. "Thank you!" She turned to where the woman in the honey salwar kameez had been standing, but she had already disappeared.

The Squad started walking in the direction the woman had suggested, passing restaurants, convenience stores, hair salons, and clothing stores.

"Look at all the colors and detailing!" Monica said, stopping before a stone window where a mannequin was draped in a dark red lehenga.

"That's a wedding gown," Hudson said, nudging her along. He was nervous about the time. They had been walking for nearly ten minutes, with no sign of a grocery or spice shop in sight. Hudson looked at his phone again—it was quickly nearing two thirty.

"And look at all that gold!" Relly said, stopping in front of an Indian jewelry shop. "Is it real?"

"I think so," Hudson said, also pausing to take a look. But he quickly started moving again. "I think we need to ask someone else."

April asked a young man, who had no idea what she was talking about, and Monica asked at a convenience store. The manager there had also never heard of the shop. Hudson asked at an Indian restaurant, where the host said he was heading in the wrong direction.

Just when Hudson was tempted to give up, a Sikh man with a pistachio-green turban stepped up the stairs of a basement-level electronics shop. He almost ran directly into Hudson.

"Excuse me, sir," Hudson said, taking a chance. "Would you happen to know where Sajna's Specialty Spice Shop is? We're looking for the one that has a variety of hot chilis."

"Ah, yes, hot chilis are so good," the man said. "And Sajna's is the place to find them. Here, let me show you. But come quick! I am in a rush!"

The Squad tried their best to keep up with the man, who moved deftly. He was dressed all in white, from head to toe, except for his green turban. He had a long flowing beard.

"I am Sajna's son," he said as they walked, his voice nearly getting lost in the wind. "She has the best shops in all of Queens. But not many people outside Queens know about her."

"I met her husband, G.G., recently," Hudson said, trotting to keep up. "He's your father?"

"Yes, yes, he's my father. The hot chilis keep him young." He chuckled before stopping abruptly in front of a café on a street corner.

"Go down this way, Hudson," G.G. and Sajna's son said. "You can't miss it." He started to walk back the way they had come before turning toward the Squad. "And keep it up with *Broadway Sizzlers*! My whole family loves that show."

Hudson and his friends started to run down the long street. Suddenly Hudson stopped short.

"I think we passed it," he said.

"Where?" Relly exclaimed. "There's nothing on this street except a long brick wall and the occasional empty storefront."

"But there was that small alleyway," Hudson said. "A few yards back. I think it was in there."

Sure enough, when the Squad retraced their steps, they spotted a small hanging sign poking out of an alleyway, swinging in the breeze. The clouds were just breaking apart, and the sun was coming out.

"There!" Hudson pointed at the sign. "Sajna's Specialty Spice Shop!"

They turned down the alley, where they immediately found a tiny shop. It was very narrow and filled from top to bottom with jars of spices and buckets of chilis. A few customers were just leaving as the Squad walked in.

"Hello," an older woman said, rising from her stool behind the counter. A clock behind her showed the Squad that it was almost three thirty. "I'm Sajna. How can I help you?" She looked at Monica, April, and Relly curiously, convinced they were in the wrong place.

Hudson stepped out from behind his friends. "I'm Hudson," Hudson introduced himself.

"Ah, Hudson Patel of *Broadway Sizzlers* in *my* shop!" Sajna said excitedly. "My husband loves your show." She smiled gently. "He told me he met you on Diwali."

Suddenly, G.G. himself emerged from a back room. "Hudson!" he said. "I thought I heard your voice. But I think you have come to the wrong store. We only have spices and chilis at this location. You'll want to go to the other store nearby, where my daughter is working today. It has all sorts of groceries."

"No, no," Hudson insisted. "This is the store I need." He paused before asking, "Is today your day off?"

"Yes, today is my day off. I leave my phone at home

and help out at the store some days," G.G. said.

"Ah, that's why I couldn't reach you!" Hudson said. He turned back to the matter at hand. "I need something very hot. A chili. My grandmother believes you could help." He quickly explained his predicament and how he wanted to find a chili that would particularly impress Charlie Richards. Then he remembered the grocery list and the mystery chili his grandmother had added at the end. It was still in his windbreaker pocket. "Do you have this one?" he asked, handing the crumpled paper to Sajna.

She looked at the name carefully and then looked at Hudson. "No one has ever asked for that before."

Hudson felt defeated. He visibly slumped where he was standing, and his face fell.

"But I do have it."

Hearing that, Hudson perked up again. Sajna disappeared to the back room, and G.G. smiled at the children.

"Tell me about your palates," Sajna asked, emerging again a few moments later. "How hot a chili can you handle?"

"I don't like spicy food," April said quietly. "I just don't have a taste for it."

"I like some heat," Relly said. "But some food is too hot. I'd say I'm about a medium."

"I can probably go head-to-head with Hudson," Monica

said. "My abuelita makes spicy Mexican food, so I grew up with it."

"Okay," Sajna said. "Now all of you should try this chili." She placed a green chili on a small cutting board on the counter and cut it into four pieces, handing one to each child.

April looked scared. Relly looked nervous too. But Hudson and Monica were eager to see what this chili was all about.

"Don't worry," Sajna said, particularly to April. "I promise, it won't hurt you."

"But will it be enough to impress Charlie Richards?" Hudson asked.

"Try it first and then decide," G.G. said. He winked.

Hudson bit into the chili. It was very hot, yes, but nothing he couldn't stand. Monica felt the same way.

Relly went next. "Not too bad," he said. "It's got heat, but it's tolerable."

April was now terrified.

"I can bring you a glass of milk to help if you can't handle it," Sajna said. "But I promise, you won't need it."

April looked at the chili in her hand carefully and then, without a word, bravely popped it into her mouth.

Everyone watched as she chewed, eyes closed. After

several long moments, her face slowly relaxed and she opened her eyes wide in amazement.

"It's not hot at all!" she said. "It's just right!"

"Same chili, different heat!" G.G. exclaimed.

"So it adjusts to everyone's palate?" Hudson asked, incredulous.

"Yes!" Sajna said. "Even someone who likes the hottest chilis will taste it. And the chili's taste will adjust to the other flavors you use. It will only make you sweat and cry if you like chilis that make you sweat and cry."

Hudson was sold. "I'll take it! All that you have."

"I don't have much," Sajna said. "But here you go."

Monica glanced at the clock on the wall. It was three forty-five p.m. "Hudson, we don't have a lot of time. You know how the trains can be."

Hudson quickly paid for the magical chili. "Thank you so much," he said to Sajna and G.G. "You have completed my recipe!"

"You're very welcome," Sajna said. "We will see you on FoodTube. Good luck!"

The Squad said goodbye to G.G. and Sajna and left the shop in a hurry, retracing their steps. They made two wrong turns on their way back, but they finally found themselves at the Roosevelt Avenue/Seventy-Fourth Street Station.

"The train is here!" Hudson said, hurrying his friends along. "Let's take it!"

They pushed their way into a crowded subway car. It was standing room only. Outside, the various neighborhoods of Queens rushed by. In their excitement, none of them realized until the doors were closing at the fourth stop—Corona Plaza—that they were heading farther into Queens, not back into Manhattan where they needed to be.

"Hudson," Monica said. "We're going the wrong way! We're going to end up all the way at the end of the line in Flushing!"

"We are?" Hudson said, confused, making his way over to the map.

But Relly took over. "We are!" he said. He pointed at the map. "We've got to change trains at Willets Point. We can probably hop on the express train from there. It will be worth the wait, I think."

"Okay," Hudson said, thinking for a moment that he wished he could call G.G. But G.G. had left his phone at home, so he couldn't ask him for a ride. And navigating the roads could take longer than waiting for the train, especially when the train would drop them directly in Times Square, where he needed to be.

The local 7 train passed by Citi Field, where the Mets played. "Let's go, Yankees!" someone at the far end of the car yelled. Some people, clearly Yankees fans, cheered, while others, Mets fans, jeered. The Squad ignored the noise and jumped off the train, searching for the platform that would put them on the express train back to Times Square. It didn't take long to find it, but it took nearly ten minutes—an eternity—for the train to arrive.

"Stand clear of the closing doors," April, Relly, and Monica said cheerfully in time with the automated voice of the train as they settled into seats. Hudson, increasingly nervous about the time, looked at them with a bit of irritation.

Relly saw Hudson look at the time again on his phone: 4:35 p.m. "Don't worry, Hudson," he said. "We'll make it."

Hudson nodded without a word. At Queensboro Plaza, the express train joined the local track, and two stops later, the last one before the train went under the East River and back into Manhattan, there was a delay.

"What could possibly be wrong now?" Hudson was exasperated. He checked the time again. There was just under an hour until the competition started at six, and he had to be there before that.

"The next stop, Grand Central, will be the last stop on this 7 train," the subway conductor announced without further explanation. "Again, Grand Central will be the last stop."

"We'll have to take the shuttle from there," April said. "We'll make it."

The train started to move again. Hudson got up from his seat and slung his backpack, filled with ingredients he would need for the competition, over his shoulder and stood in front of the door, ready to run. His friends joined him without a word. As soon as the train pulled into Grand Central, they were off.

"Excuse us," April bellowed from the back of the group. Tourists and locals alike made space.

"Aren't you the kids from *Our Time*?" a woman asked as they ran past. April stopped for a moment and curtsied. "Yes, ma'am!" she said. "Thanks for noticing, but we're in a huge rush. We've got a cupcake competition to win!"

The Squad was running toward the shuttle when an announcement stopped them short. "The shuttle to Times Square is delayed," the voice said.

"We're going to have to run!" Hudson shouted. "We can't waste any time!"

The Squad bolted up the stairs that led them to the main hall of Grand Central. They were too busy pushing past all the people to take in the grandeur of the space, not the celestial ceiling overhead or the famous gold clock at the center.

Once outside, they ran as fast as they could to Times

Square, Hudson in the lead. It was about a mile west on Forty-Second Street. In some sections, they even ran in the street, weaving between the cars parked at stoplights. Finally, they made it to the Marriott Marquis hotel and followed signs to a grand ballroom, where the competition would take place. Velvet ropes blocked off the entrance.

Hudson, breathless, approached a security guard. "I'm Hudson Patel," he said. "I'm here for the cupcake competition."

Seventeen

The security guard looked over Hudson and his friends.

"Hudson Patel," he said. "You nearly got disqualified. You had barely ten minutes to spare before we called you a no-show."

"Well, he's here," April said, catching her breath and pushing her way to the front of her group of friends. "And he's ready to bake!"

The security guard grinned at April, who was hardly half his height.

"All right," he said, unhooking the velvet rope so Hudson could pass through. "You can go into the room."

April, Relly, and Monica were ready to follow Hudson through, but the security guard cut them off.

"Only Hudson goes that way," he said. "Are you his friends?"

"Yes," Relly said confidently. "His best friends."

"You must be Relly Morton," the security guard said, consulting the names on the list. "And you two have to be Monica Garcia and April DaSilva. You can head that way," he said, gesturing to another entrance down the hall. "Hudson's family are already seated there."

"Good luck, Hudson," Monica said, reaching over the velvet rope to give him a quick hug. "But you don't need it." April also gave him a hug and Relly a fist bump before they went their separate ways.

Once inside the room, it took Hudson a moment to get his bearings. He was used to stage lights, but these cameras and television lights left him unsteady. He nearly tripped over camera wires in front of him, when a lady in a watermelon-pink dress grabbed his arm.

"Hudson Patel!" she exclaimed. "I'm so happy to see you!" She ushered him to a station set up with an oven and a stove, as well as spatulas, mixers, and cutting boards. "You can set up here. Put all your special ingredients on the counter, where the cameras can see them. We've provided all the mixing bowls, spatulas, and other tools that you'll need. And that large pantry has all the staples, like sugar, flour, milk, and even yogurt. Good luck!"

With that, she was gone.

Hudson looked around the room quickly. There were two other baking stations, for the two other contestants. A girl much taller than Hudson was to his left, and a boy a few years younger was to his right. Hudson waved at the girl when she looked at him. She nodded at him but did not return his smile.

Okay, he said to himself. *I guess I'm not here to make friends.*

Hudson quickly set up his ingredients on the counter. He spotted his mother waving at him. She called over the security guard who had let Hudson into the ballroom and handed him something. She gestured toward Hudson as she spoke to the man.

"Looks like you forgot this at home." The security guard handed over Hudson's white apron. "It's nice to have a family that looks out for you."

"Yes, and friends to help too," Hudson responded.

He looked up at the audience again, squinting through the bright lights. He could see his parents, as well as his nani, his brother, and his baby sister. Next to them were April, Relly, and Monica. They all waved at him excitedly.

Hudson was just buttoning the last button on his apron

when Charlie Richards entered the ballroom, also nearly tripping over camera wires and shielding his face from the lights with his hands.

"Oh my gosh, it's Charlie Richards!" the boy who was Hudson's other competitor shouted. He started to run around his table in Charlie's direction, but the security guard stopped him.

"There will be plenty of time to meet Charlie later," the guard said, ushering the boy back to his table.

But Charlie, charmed, walked right over to the boy. "Hi there," he said. "I'm Charlie. I'm very excited to taste what you make this evening."

"Hi, Charlie," the boy said. "May I wear your cowboy hat?"

Charlie laughed. "Maybe after the competition," he said.

Hudson thought the boy was going to faint.

Charlie walked over to the girl next. She was nearly as tall as he was. Again, he introduced himself. She extended her hand for a formal handshake.

Finally, Charlie walked over to Hudson. "Hi, Hudson," he said. "It's great to finally meet you. I'm looking forward to your cupcake."

"Thanks, Charlie," Hudson said. "I really think you're going to like it."

Charlie laughed. The woman in pink came by and ushered him to the front of the ballroom. Hudson snickered.

She reminded him of Claudia. "We're ready to go live in thirty seconds, Charlie," she said.

Charlie got into place. He didn't even adjust his cowboy hat or his jacket. He simply relaxed into his stance, his thumbs in his belt loops, and his feet, clad in cowboy boots, slightly askew. He was as cool and calm as ever. The cameras started rolling, and before Hudson knew it, Charlie was announcing the start of the competition.

"Good evening, food fans!" he began. "I'm Charlie Richards, and you're watching Bake It Till You Make It, live from Times Square in New York City! This year, only kids under the age of fifteen could enter the competition. We had many, many entries, but we narrowed it down to three finalists, who will make their final creations live tonight. As you may know, I enjoy tasting family recipes of all sorts, so we stuck to that theme for the competition. The instructions: make a cupcake that includes flavors from their family recipes.

"Here are our three contestants," Charlie continued, turning toward the tables.

"First we have Elena, age fourteen, from Temple, Texas. Her family originates from Bulgaria." Elena, her strawberry-blond hair pulled back in two tight French braids, smiled widely for the camera.

"Next," Charlie continued, "we have eleven-year-old Haruto, who is joining us tonight from Saint Louis, Missouri. His cupcake is influenced by Japanese cuisine."

Haruto smiled so wide and waved so eagerly that Hudson wondered how he wasn't in pain.

"And last but not least," Charlie said, "we have Hudson, age thirteen, from right here in New York City. Some of you may know him from his own FoodTube show, *Broadway Sizzlers*, or from his Broadway show, *Our Time*. Hudson's family hails from India."

Hudson held a hand up to the camera and grinned. Then he spotted April, Monica, and Relly in the audience, bouncing up and down in front of their chairs. Hudson knew they were excited for him—and for the free plug for *Our Time*.

"With that, let's get started," Charlie said. He turned to the children again. "You can use any of the ingredients you brought with you, along with the appliances and general ingredients we provided. If you have any problems, let us know." He looked over each of the contestants quickly. "You'll have two hours. Are you ready?"

Hudson gave a thumbs-up, and Elena simply nodded. Haruto eagerly shouted, "Ready!"

"Ready, set, bake!"

Everyone immediately got to work, pulling out mixing bowls, pouring flour, and, in Hudson's case, cutting fruit—mangoes, specifically.

Charlie went from station to station, observing but not interrupting the work. He would talk to the camera from time to time, quietly, away from the contestants, almost like a sports commentator at a game.

The live audience also watched eagerly. Hudson's nani was peering closely at the ingredients on Hudson's table. "It looks like he found the chili!" she said.

"He did!" Monica said, turning to face her. "It's quite special."

Nani smiled. "You three are very good friends to Hudson. Thank you for helping him."

"You're very special too," April said.

Back at their baking stations, the three contestants were putting the finishing touches on their cupcake creations. Charlie was already eyeing the creations curiously. He was particularly drawn to Hudson's station, where the green chili caught his eye. He watched closely as Hudson, who had taken quite a lot of care in making the structure stick, placed a chili on his final cupcake, just as the allotted two hours ran out.

"Time's up! Let's check out the cupcake creations!" Charlie said to the cameras before turning to the kids. "Here we go. First we'll take a look at Elena's creation. What have you made?"

"I modified the traditional Bulgarian recipe for custard-filled pastry horns, or funiiki s krem," Elena said. "I made it into the shape of a cupcake, filled the center with custard, closed off the cupcake, and then added more custard, rather than frosting. On top, I have added a chocolate-covered strawberry, along with cinnamon. It is seemingly simple, but it is something that would sell well in Times Square to a variety of people."

"It looks beautiful," Charlie said. The camera zoomed in on one of Elena's cupcakes. He took a big bite. "Mmmm." He chewed carefully, analyzing the flavors. "This is very good, but the custard from the inside is dripping down my hands."

Elena, who had looked very sure of herself moments before, suddenly looked surprised, even nervous.

"Excellent effort," Charlie said, wiping his hands clean. "But let's see what our other two contestants have."

He moved on to Haruto's table. "What do we have here?" Charlie asked.

Haruto began talking very animatedly as he explained what he had made. "I used wagashi, a traditional Japanese sweet, to make this cupcake," he said. "It's like marzipan. If you make it right, it's very malleable and you can shape it into anything you want. See? I made a lemon-flavored base, with a lavender-infused frosting and traditional wagashi on top. It's shaped like an iris, see?"

Charlie picked up one of Haruto's cupcakes. "This cupcake is certainly very beautiful," he said. "I almost don't want to eat it." He looked down at Haruto, who was beaming at him.

"But you have to, Charlie," he said. "Please, taste it!"

"Well, if you insist," Charlie said. He took a big bite of the cupcake, purple icing getting caught in his beard and mustache.

"Excellent job, Haruto," he said. "I love the way you used the wagashi to make the cupcake structure, and it's really impressive that you got it in the proper shape in such a short time. But, I wonder, is it too sweet?"

Haruto's smile faded as Charlie set the remainder of the cupcake down and took a drink of water.

"We have one more contestant," Charlie said to the camera as he walked over to Hudson's table. "Let's see what Hudson has made."

He stood next to Hudson, who was suddenly nervous. His cupcakes were bigger than the others', and he hoped it wasn't too unwieldy.

"So, Hudson, tell us about your cupcake recipe," Charlie said.

Hudson took a deep breath and blew his bangs out of his eyes. "I call it the Spice of Life," he said.

"Oh really?" Charlie said. "That's great that you named

it. And I'm guessing that name has something to do with this green chili on top."

"That's right," Hudson said, suddenly feeling confident and comfortable, even excited. "But first, let me tell you about the rest of the cupcake. The base is a play on gulab jamun, a traditional Indian dessert that consists of fried dough flavored with cardamom and saffron and then drowned in a very sweet syrup. I added mango and chili powder and skipped the syrup."

"Chili powder?" Charlie asked.

"Yes!" Hudson said. "Chili powder. I know how much you like spices."

"Okay," Charlie said. "You have my attention. I can see how mango and chili powder would go together."

"Between the first and second levels is a layer of pista barfi—pistachio barfi. It's got milk, ghee, pistachio extract, and chopped pistachios. It's thinner than traditional barfi, and I added it for both color and flavor—and to help the layers stick together.

"Between the second and third layers is a layer of shrikhand. It's a creamy dessert made of mango, saffron, sugar, and yogurt.

"I drizzled the top layer with imli, a sweet-and-tangy sauce that is made of tamarind and prunes," Hudson continued.

"I thought it was chocolate." Charlie was clearly intrigued.

"On top of that is a piece of rose barfi—it's similar to the pistachio barfi, but without the pistachio flavor. The pink color comes from food coloring."

"And what about the thin silver layer on top?" Charlie asked. "Can you eat that?"

"Yes!" Hudson said. "That's edible silver paper. You'll find it on a lot of Indian desserts."

"And the chili on top?"

"That, Charlie, is the pièce de résistance," Hudson said with his best French accent. "Without it, the cupcake would just be a cupcake."

"It's got a lot of other things going for it," Charlie said. He eyed the cupcakes curiously and then picked one up. "I do love hot chilis," he added.

He took a big bite of the cupcake, getting some of every layer in his mouth. Then he bit off half the chili.

Hudson watched him carefully. He was not nervous anymore. After the experience with his friends at Sajna's shop that afternoon, he was confident Charlie would get just the right amount of heat and flavor with the cupcake to suit his palate.

Charlie kept chewing and then took another bite. Once he finished, he turned to Hudson. "How did you do that?"

he asked, incredulous. "It's the exact perfect proportion of sweet to savory to hot spice!"

"It's magic," Hudson said. He winked.

Charlie finished eating his second bite and then put the cupcake down. "You did a really excellent job, Hudson," he said. "But I'm not sure this will sell in Times Square. It suits my palate, but it's likely too hot for many people, especially kids."

"But that's the beauty of it!" Hudson said. "It really is magic. That chili adjusts to each individual person's taste."

Charlie looked at him, speechless.

"I'm serious," Hudson said. "Here, have someone else taste it."

Charlie looked around at the crew. He gestured for the security guard and the woman in pink to join him.

"I don't like spicy food at all," the woman said.

"I can only handle a little," the man chimed in. "It upsets my stomach."

"You'll be fine," Hudson said. "I promise."

The guard and the woman looked at each other and each took a bite of extra chilis that Hudson held out to them. Sure enough, they were impressed.

"I can't taste anything but a little bit of a punch!" the woman said.

"For me, it's a bit of heat, but only for a moment. It's

nice," the guard said. "It wakes you up, that's for sure."

"That's amazing," Charlie said.

"There's one more thing about the cupcake," Hudson said. "I can't forget this part. Each section of the cupcake represents something special."

"What do you mean?" Charlie asked.

"The base—the gulab jamun—is my family. They are my rock. They encourage me and inspire me in every way. The layers in between represent my friends—April, Relly, and Monica. They make life fun and help me hold things together."

"And the chili?" Charlie asked.

"Well, that's for the magic in life," Hudson said. "But really it's for my nani, my grandmother, who always encourages me to follow my heart." He paused and looked for his family in the crowd, spotting his nani drying her tears on her intricate Kashmiri shawl. "She's quite a spicy character herself—you should see her dance!"

Hudson beamed as Charlie considered all three cupcake entries carefully. He took one more bite of each. With Hudson's he made sure to get all the flavors at once. He even took an extra bite of the green chili.

"Okay, I need a few minutes to consider who our winner is," Charlie said to the crowd in the room. He turned to the cameras. "We'll announce the winner of Bake It Till You Make It shortly."

Charlie disappeared into the pantry. "I think he needs some space," Hudson's father whispered to his wife. Hudson leaned against the counter of his makeshift baking station as he waited. Haruto sampled his own cupcake, and Elena stood quietly.

Finally, Charlie emerged again. Everyone turned to him eagerly.

"It looks like we have our winner," Charlie said. "Congratulations, Hudson! Your cupcake is not only tasty and unique, drawing on your culture and heritage, but it has so much symbolism and significance. You're going to be selling your cupcake creation right here in Times Square next summer!"

"Thanks!" Hudson exclaimed.

Charlie Richards ended the show. He thanked Elena and Haruto for their participation. "Keep up the good baking. And keep exploring all sorts of flavors. You both did an excellent job!" he said. He placed his cowboy hat on Haruto's head, and he shook Elena's hand. "Until next time," he said, tilting his head toward the camera.

The Patel family stepped forward and surrounded the Squad.

"What an excellent evening!" Nani exclaimed. "All that hard work paid off. I know it wasn't easy, but you did it, and all with your friends' help!"

"And yours," Hudson said. "Thanks, Nani, for helping me out and for reminding me what matters most."

"So, what's for dinner?" Hudson's father asked, ruffling his son's hair.

"I've been cooking all day," Nani said. "I made a feast. I finally got around to making that Diwali dinner. Better late than never!"

The group made its way toward the doors and down the escalators that took them to the ground floor. The Squad stepped into the giant revolving doors together, just as Claudia and Artie tried to come in the opposite way. Jimmy stood aside and laughed at the sight. Finally, everyone joined him outside.

"Congratulations, Hudson! Cupcake baker extraordinaire!" Artie's arms were flying through the air as he beamed at Hudson. His scarf was coming undone. He wasn't just happy for Hudson's success—it was clear that tonight's free press for *Our Time* would be a huge boost for the show.

"We watched it live on the TV in my office," Jimmy explained. "You really did a great job, Hudson. I can't wait to try that cupcake!"

"Yes, we all have to try the cupcake!" Claudia exclaimed. "Maybe you can bring some samples to the Fall Festival at Duffy Square? I'm sure all of Broadway will want to try them between performances."

"Well, right now these kids need food to keep them going!" Nani exclaimed. "Come, let's get to that Diwali meal. You are all welcome to join us," she added, turning to Claudia, Artie, and Jimmy Onions. "Space might be tight, but I promise you it will be worth it."

Hudson grabbed his nani's hand and gave it a tight squeeze. "Thank you for all your help," he said.

"Oh, Hudson, that's what family—and friends—are for."

Hudson squeezed her hand again. "You should be a guest on *Broadway Sizzlers*," he said.

"I'm too shy for that," she protested.

"No, you're not! And we could do another show with all the grandparents—you, Monica's abuelita, and Relly's grandpa Gregory. And another show with my mom and dad. And even one with Sudhir!"

"And what about us?" Monica interrupted. "Can't Relly, April, and I be on your show?"

Hudson was beaming. "Of course you can be on the show. You'll be the first ones. Well, after my nani."

As they started walking away from the hotel, the Squad noticed a familiar figure approaching.

"Uh, Artie," Relly said uncertainly as he caught their director's attention.

"What's up?" Artie asked. He followed Relly's gaze.

It was their producer, Slick Rick Gallo, dressed in a cranberry-red suit and matching tie paired with a lemon-yellow shirt. He was wearing his signature plum glasses with the cotton-candy-pink lenses. A white rose sat perfectly in his breast pocket.

"Artie, this is brilliant!" Rick whooped, the white rose bopping in his breast pocket with his every move. "Have Hudson win a baking competition! This is going to boost our ticket sales for sure! I always knew you were a genius!"

Artie was silent, stunned by Rick's appearance—and compliments.

"You've got it all wrong, Mr. Gallo," Monica chirped.

"Yeah," April chimed in. "Hudson did this all on his own!"

"He did?" Rick adjusted the pink-lensed glasses on his nose.

"He did," Artie said, finally recovered. "He's incredibly talented, and we're incredibly lucky to have him in our show."

Hudson, who had been staring at his shoes, looked over at Artie, who was beaming at him.

"I really mean that, Hudson," Artie said.

"Thanks, Artie. I'm really proud to be part of the show. It's a great team," Hudson said.

Rick turned to Hudson. "You're a big star now, Hudson. A multifaceted, multitalented star. We'll get the entire cast and crew together tomorrow at the Ethel Merman and celebrate!"

"Thank you, Mr. Gallo." Hudson winked at his friends.

Back in Times Square, Hudson, Monica, Relly, and April ran ahead of the rest of the group. The energy was, as always, electric. "It's our time!" they shouted together, as they grabbed each other's hands.

Monica tapped Hudson on the shoulder and pointed up at a large screen. Hudson's face flashed across it. *Congratulations to Hudson Patel, the winner of Bake It Till You Make It! You've got the Spice of Life!*

Hudson beamed. Tonight he was the biggest star on Broadway.

Eighteen

A few days later, Hudson awoke feeling more refreshed than he had in a very long time. It was Saturday, the day the Squad would join other Broadway casts in showcasing their work in a Fall Festival. Hudson had been so focused on the cupcake competition that he had nearly forgotten all about it.

He quickly got dressed. In the kitchen, Nani was cleaning up the last of the pots from the night before.

"Good morning, beta!" she exclaimed. "How are you feeling today?"

Hudson took a moment to consider his response. "I feel amazing," he said.

"Everything is better with your friends now, I hope," Nani said.

"You know, Nani, despite all the stress of the last few weeks, my friends stuck by me. That means a lot. I really enjoy performing on Broadway, and I want to keep doing it."

Now Nani leaned in closely. "How are you going to juggle all your interests, beta?" Hudson noticed the slight smile on her mouth, the twinkle in her eye.

"I can do both," he said. "I love the community that the show and Broadway present to me. And I heard what Artie told Slick Rick the other night: I'm talented. I realized that I wouldn't be here—on Broadway—if I weren't. So I'm committed to the show. And to my friends. I couldn't do it all without them, and I wouldn't want to."

Hudson looked around the kitchen. He picked up an avocado from the fruit bowl. "I still love baking, but it's something I do mostly on my own. It's fun to experiment with the flavors and build new things, but I don't know whether I've done a good job until I share my creations with other people. So I can do both. And my friends are always willing to step in and help. They remind me that I'm enough."

"Good, beta." Nani was smiling fully now.

Hudson gave her a big hug. "You should change," he said. "It's chilly today, and I want you to come to the Fall Festival."

"I can come to the performance today?" Nani was bouncing on her toes, her hands clasped at her chest.

"Yes, but you may need to wear a coat instead of a shawl. I don't want you to catch a cold."

"Look at you, all concerned about your nani!"

Nani hurried out of the room to put on a heavier sweater, while Hudson gathered up some samples of his winning cupcakes, along with a few other treats he had recently made.

A short while later, the entire Patel family was in Duffy Square, near the TKTS line again. Hudson looked for the Squad.

"Hudson, we're over here!" It was Monica, who had brought her abuelita. Relly was there, too, with Grandpa Gregory, his brother, and his mom.

"Oh, good! You all brought your families!" April exclaimed. Her own parents walked closely behind her. "That's so great!"

"Are you kids ready?" Nani asked. "I hear you have some competition here."

"Yeah, it turns out the *Move It!* kids are performing today too," April said.

"Yes, they are, but let's have some fun today. Okay?" Monica said.

"Deal!"

The Squad's families made their way to the sweeping red steps at one end of Duffy Square.

"Kids, you're up first." Claudia's voice boomed over the city noise and the crowd gathering in the square. Artie and Jimmy were with her.

"We're ready!" Hudson bellowed. "We're starting with 'Growing Up in the 'Burbs,' right?"

"Yes!" Claudia said. "Now, places!"

The Squad made it through the song seamlessly. The crowd's applause was stimulating. Hudson hadn't been so excited about performing in a long time.

"Wait a minute," Relly said. "What happened to Tabitha?" The *Move It!* cast, dressed in their animal costumes, was just starting to perform the lead song of their upcoming show.

Artie chuckled. Everyone turned to look at him.

"Well, kids, she backed out of *Move It!*"

"What?" the Squad shouted in unison.

"Yes." Claudia jumped in. "She even backed out of her big tell-all interview."

"She did?" Monica was stunned.

"During rehearsals, she got stuck on a floating crystal ball," Jimmy said. He was clearly trying not to laugh.

"And one of the understudies screamed so loud from a seat in the audience when the interactive spider features tickled her legs that you couldn't hear Tabitha's solo," Artie added. He was also trying not to laugh.

"So she quit?" Monica asked.

"Yes, she quit," a voice behind her said. It was Slick Rick. "She claimed that the Broadhurst must be haunted." He slid his glasses down his nose and raised his eyebrows as he looked over the Squad. "She broke the news just before backing out of her tell-all interview with *Good Morning America*. Now it's not clear that *Move It!* will open at all." He looked at the Squad closely. "I'm glad to know that no one in your cast is a quitter." He looked directly at Hudson and winked.

Hudson winked back and then turned to watch the *Move It!* cast wrap up its song. "I have an idea," he said. "What if we perform with the kids from *Move It!*?"

Claudia looked pleased. "I think that would be lovely," she said.

"There's got to be a song we all know," Relly said.

"How about 'Somewhere' from *West Side Story*?" Monica suggested.

"That's the perfect song!" April said. "*Hold my hand and we're halfway there . . . ,*" she sang.

The Squad approached the other cast. "Hi!" Hudson said. "I'm Hudson. We'd really like to sing with you. Do you want to sing 'Somewhere' from *West Side Story* with us?"

"Oh my gosh, that would be *so* great!" one of the kids, dressed as a llama, said.

"We'd love to perform with you!" said another, who was dressed as a giraffe. "But can we sing one of the songs from *Our Time*? We all had to sing 'Finally Found' for our *Move It!* audition. We love that song, and your show."

The Squad was surprised. They hadn't expected the other kids to be fans.

Hudson broke the silence. "Sure." All the children found their way to the middle of the square.

"Monica, you should start. It's really your song," Hudson said.

"No, Hudson." Monica smiled. "I think you should start it today."

Hudson looked back up at the electronic billboard, which still featured his face for winning the cupcake competition. Without another word, he stepped forward and began to sing. After the first line, the rest of the Squad joined in, and then the *Move It!* cast rounded it out.

> *I am finally found*
> *Finally free*
> *Content and at peace from the wars*
> *That have built up inside of me*
> *I am finally found*
> *By a wish that came true:*
> *That someday I'd be finally found by you.*

At the end of the song, there were several moments of silence, followed by a thunder of applause. All the kids joined hands and bowed together.

Hudson walked over to his nani, who was holding the boxes of treats he had brought for everyone to try. He opened the box full of his winning cupcakes. He offered them to the Squad and the other casts that were there for the Fall Festival.

"This is it," he said, gesturing to all the people gathered and more broadly at the nearby theaters and his Broadway friends around him. "This community is the Spice of Life."

Acknowledgments

THANK YOU, MANDY, FOR YOUR FAITH IN ME AND for trusting me to help bring Hudson's story to life. Your passion for creative work is exhilarating. Working on this project has fulfilled a lifelong dream—writing a work of fiction. I am very honored to be part of the #FearlessSquad!

Thanks also to Aly Heller and the rest of the team at Simon & Schuster. Your feedback kept me on track, and I appreciate your kindness and patience in delivering it.

Thank you, Jess Regel of Helm Literary, for your guidance. I am grateful for your time and belief in me.

Thank you, Grace Williams. You are a true friend, remembering my dreams when I had set them aside myself.

Thank you to my parents. Your stories and experiences helped me navigate and craft Hudson's, and I look forward to continuing to learn more from you—I know there's so much more.

Thank you, Robert, for brainstorming with me from the beginning. I worried that I would not have the bandwidth for this project, but you helped me see the bigger picture, that this book is a once-in-a-lifetime opportunity. You saw my potential, resilience, and talent when I could not see them in myself. And I love that our first "real" vacation together was a two-day whirlwind trip to see Mandy in *Hamilton* on Broadway.

And thank you to New York City, a magical place that was my home for a dozen years. You excite and motivate in so many ways.

—*Sushil*

CURIOSITY IS SUCH A WONDERFUL THING! I HOPE this book reminds you, the reader, that it's okay to pursue multiple things! It's okay to step out of your comfort zone, and to put yourself out there in different ways. That is what makes you uniquely you!

Sushil Cheema, this collaboration has been a total joy. Your talent is only matched by your beautiful heart. Thank you for the endless Zooms and willingness to leap with me.

Mom and Dad, thank you for always listening to my stories, and for your belief in me. Thank you for taking me to the library as a kid, so I would discover my love of reading.

My wonderful editor, Alyson Heller, thank you for your guidance. So happy we've been on this incredible ride together. Here's to creating many more Broadway adventures!

My agent, Jessica Regal, at Helm Literary, thank you

for your infinite wisdom and guidance. Together, everything is possible!

Thank you, Saira Rao and Carey Albertine, at In This Together Media for believing in all things FEARLESS! You inspire me!

Ally Shuster, thanks for the endless check-ins and for your faith in this series.

Geraldine Rodriguez, thank you for hitting it out of the park once again.

Thank you to everyone at Simon & Shuster!

To my Fearless Squad, Lou D'ambrosio, Alexa D'ambrosio, and Mark Bonchek. You continue to inspire me! No pare sigue sigue!! I HELD your hand in mine, and together we will change the world!

And to my beautiful family, Douglas and Maribelle: Te quiero hasta la luna.

 —Mandy

ABOUT THE AUTHORS

MANDY GONZALEZ possesses one of the most powerful and versatile contemporary voices of our time. Currently starring in *Hamilton* as Angelica Schuyler, Mandy originated and starred as Nina Rosario in the Tony Award-winning *In the Heights*, for which she received a Drama Desk Award, and starred as Elphaba in the Broadway production of *Wicked*.

Mandy has performed with symphonies around the world, and made her Carnegie Hall debut with the New York Pops in 2020.

Her debut middle-grade novel, *Fearless*, published in 2021. Mandy is the proud founder of #FearlessSquad—a global social media movement for inclusiveness and positivity, empowering people to be their best selves.

SUSHIL PREET K. CHEEMA is first-generation American with roots in India and in East Africa. Her interest in storytelling began in elementary school, leading her to a career in journalism. She has been a freelancer for the *New York Times* and a staff multimedia reporter for the *Wall Street Journal*. Now based in her hometown of Tampa, Florida, she continues to weave storytelling into her work as an executive coach. She is forever grateful to her parents and her partner for their love and support.